TOKYO UENO STATION

TOKYO UENO STATION

Yu Miri

TRANSLATED BY MORGAN GILES

RIVERHEAD BOOKS   NEW YORK   2020

RIVERHEAD BOOKS
An imprint of Penguin Random House LLC
penguinrandomhouse.com

English translation copyright © 2019 by Morgan Giles
First published in Japan by Kawade Shobō Shinsha as
JR Ueno-eki Koen-guchi, Tokyo, 2014
First published in Great Britain in paperback in
English by Tilted Axis Press, London, 2019
First American edition published by Riverhead Books, 2020

LIBRARY OF CONGRESS CATALOGING-IN-PUBLICATION DATA

Names: Yū, Miri, 1968– author. | Giles, Morgan, translator.
Title: Tokyo Ueno station / Yu Miri ; translated by Morgan Giles.
Other titles: JR Ueno-eki kōenguchi. English
Description: First American edition. | New York : Riverhead Books, 2020. |
First published in Japan by Kawade Shobō Shinsha as *JR Ueno-eki
Koen-guchi*, Tokyo, 2014. First published in Great Britain in paperback
in English by Tilted Axis Press, London, 2019. | Translated from the Japanese.
Identifiers: LCCN 2019052105 (print) | LCCN 2019052106 (ebook) |
ISBN 9780593088029 (hardcover) | ISBN 9780593187531 (ebook)
Subjects: LCSH: Homeless persons—Japan—Fiction. | Working
class—Japan—Fiction. | Parks—Japan—Tokyo—Fiction. | Japan—Social
conditions—21st century—Fiction. | Tokyo (Japan)—Fiction. |
Ueno Kōen (Tokyo, Japan)—Fiction. | GSAFD: Ghost stories.
Classification: LCC PL865.U28 J7813 2020 (print) |
LCC PL865.U28 (ebook) | DDC 895.63/6—dc23
LC record available at https://lccn.loc.gov/2019052105
LC ebook record available at https://lccn.loc.gov/2019052106

Printed in the United States of America
3 5 7 9 10 8 6 4 2

BOOK DESIGN BY LUCIA BERNARD

TOKYO UENO STATION

There's that sound again.

That sound—

I hear it.

But I don't know if it's in my ears or in my mind.

I don't know if it's inside me or outside.

I don't know when it was or who it was either.

Is that important?

Was it?

Who was it?

I used to think life was like a book: you turn the first page, and there's the next, and as you go on turning page after page, eventually you reach the last one. But life is nothing like a story in a book. There may be words, and the pages may be numbered, but there is no plot. There may be an ending, but there is no end.

Left behind—

Like a sculpted tree on the vacant land where a rotted house has been torn down.

Like the water in a vase after wilted flowers have been removed.

Left behind.

But then what of me remains here?

A sense of tiredness.

I was always tired.

There was never a time I was not tired.

Not when life had its claws in me and not when I escaped from it.

I did not live with intent, I only lived.

But that's all over now.

I watch slowly, like always.

It's not the same scene, but it's similar.

Somewhere in this dull scene, there's pain.

In this seemingly familiar time, there are moments that hurt.

I look closer.

There are lots of people.

Each and every one different.

Each and every one with different minds, different faces, bodies, and hearts.

I know that, of course.

But seen from a distance, they all look just the same, or similar.

Each and every face looks like nothing so much as a small pool of water.

I'm watching for myself on the day I first set foot on the platform at Ueno Station, in the throng of people waiting for the Yamanote Line inner-loop train to arrive.

I used to look at my appearance reflected in mirrors, glass panes, and pictures, and I had no confidence in myself. I do not think I was especially ugly, but I never had the kind of looks that would have attracted anyone's attention.

My reticence and incompetence troubled me more than my appearance, but worst of all was how unlucky I was.

I had no luck.

I hear that sound again. Just that sound, like it's blood coursing—like a vivid current flowing—back then I heard nothing but that sound, rushing around inside my skull, like there was a hive in my head and hundreds of bees were trying to fly out all at once, it buzzed and burned and hurt,

I could think of nothing anymore, my eyelids twitched and trembled as if they were being hit by raindrops, I clenched my fists, all the muscles in my body tensed—

It ripped me to shreds, but the sound wouldn't die.

I couldn't catch it, and trap it, or lead it far from me.

I couldn't close my ears to it, and I couldn't get away.

Ever since then that sound has lived with me.

Lived . . . ?

THE TRAIN NOW APPROACHING PLATFORM TWO IS FOR IKEBUKURO AND SHINJUKU. FOR YOUR SAFETY PLEASE STAND BEHIND THE YELLOW LINE.

———·———

If you go out the ticket gates at Ueno Station's park exit and look over the road to the grove of ginkgo trees, you'll always see homeless people there.

When I sat there, I felt like an only child who had been orphaned, despite the fact that both of my parents had lived into their nineties, never leaving their village in Sōma, Fukushima Prefecture. And following my own birth in

1933, my parents had four daughters and three sons: Haruko, Fukiko, Hideo, Naoko, Michiko, Katsuo, and Masao.

The fourteen years between Masao and me made him more like my child than my brother.

But time had passed.

And here I sat, alone, growing older—

During my brief, light slumbers, I would snore, exhausted, and when my eyes opened now and then, the netlike shadow traced by the leaves of the ginkgoes would sway, and I felt that I was wandering directionless despite being here, despite having been here in this park, for years—

"Enough." The word shot from the man who had appeared to be asleep; white smoke rose, slowly, from his mouth and nostrils. The cherry of the cigarette he held in his right hand looked like it would soon burn his fingers. Years of sweat and grime had changed the colors of his clothing beyond recognition, but with his tweed flat cap, checkered coat, and brown leather boots, he looked like an English huntsman.

A car climbed Yamashita-dōri toward Uguisudani. The lights turned green, the signal for the visually impaired bleeped, and the people coming out of the station at the park exit started to cross the road toward us.

The man leaned forward at the sight of the people crossing the road—people with beautifully decorated homes—as if he were searching for the limits of his vision, and then, hand trembling, as though this gesture took all the strength he had left, he brought the cigarette up to his mouth to inhale—his beard more white than not—then exhaled as he put the thought behind him, spreading his aged fingers to drop the cigarette, snuffing out the embers with the toe of his faded boot.

Another man, sleeping with a large translucent bag of scavenged aluminum cans tucked between his legs, clutched a clear vinyl umbrella as if it were a cane.

A woman slept prone, using a maroon backpack as a futon and her arms as a pillow, her white hair tied up with a rubber band.

The faces had changed, and the numbers had gone down.

After the asset bubble burst, the population swelled and the park was so crowded with tarp huts that you could no longer see the grass, only the paths and facilities like bathrooms and kiosks.

Whenever a member of the imperial family was due to

visit one of the park's museums or galleries, a mass eviction would occur; we would be forced to take down our tents and be driven out of the park, and on returning after dark we would find new signs reading LAWN MAINTENANCE IN PROGRESS—PLEASE KEEP OFF THE GRASS, further restricting the space we could take.

Many of the homeless in Ueno Imperial Gift Park came from the northeast.

"The Gateway to the North"—during the postwar economic boom, young people from the northeast had taken overnight trains en masse to search for work in the capital, and Ueno was the place they disembarked. And when they went back home for the holidays with only the bags they could carry, Ueno was where they caught their trains.

Fifty years had passed; parents and siblings had died, and the family homes we should have returned to had disappeared for those of us who passed our days in this park.

The homeless people sitting on the concrete enclosure around the grove of ginkgo trees are all either sleeping or eating.

A man wearing a dark blue baseball cap pulled low over his eyes and a khaki button-down shirt was eating a bento off the lap of his black trousers.

We never lacked for food.

There was an unspoken agreement with the many long-established restaurants in Ueno: after they closed for the night, many places did not lock their back doors. Inside, clearly set apart from the food waste, the unsold food would have been neatly portioned out and bagged.

Convenience stores, too, would put bentos, sandwiches, and pastries past their best-before date in the area next to the dumpster, so if we went before the trash was collected, we could claim anything we wanted. When it was nice out, we had to eat the food right away, but when it was cold, we could keep it in our huts for days and heat it up on camping stoves.

Every Wednesday and Sunday, the Tokyo Metropolitan Festival Hall provided us with curry and rice; on Fridays it was the End of the Earth Mission Church; and on Saturdays the Missionaries of Charity distributed food. Missionaries of Charity was Mother Teresa's, and End of the Earth Mission Church was Korean. They had banners that read REPENT, FOR THE KINGDOM OF HEAVEN IS AT HAND and young girls with long hair who sang hymns and strummed guitars—women with frizzy perms stirring giant pots with ladles—homeless people would come from as far away as Shinjuku, Ikebukuro, and Asakusa, so often the line would be long, nearly five hundred strong. When the hymns and sermons were done with, they distributed the food. Kimchi rice with ham and cheese and sausage, rice and beans with yakisoba, sweet bread with coffee . . . Praise the Lord, praise the Lord, praise the Lord's name, hallelujah, hallelujah—

"I'm hungry, Mama."

"You want some of this?"

"Don't want it."

"Well, then Mama's gonna eat it all."

"No, Mama, don't!"

A little girl of about five years, in a short-sleeved dress pale pink as cherry blossoms, walks with her head turned to look up at her mother, whose body-hugging, leopard-print dress suggests a job in the nighttime economy.

Another young woman in a navy-blue suit passes them, her heels clicking.

Just then a sudden downpour strikes the deep canopy of the cherry trees and falls onto the pavement, leaving its dark footprints here and there.

Even in the rain, the stream of people never stops.

Under their umbrellas side by side, two old women in loose blouses and identical black slacks chat as they walk.

"It was seventy-two this morning, wasn't it?"

"Mm-hmm."

"You can't say it's cold, but it is chilly. I feel like I could freeze!"

"What a chilly rain!"

"You know, Ryuji won't stop going on about his step-mother's cooking."

"Oh, how dreadful for you."

"He thinks I could learn a few things from her."

"So awful, isn't it, this rain."

"And the rainy season's just begun. We've got another month of this to look forward to."

"Are the hydrangeas in bloom now, do you think?"

"Oh, not yet."

"And the Japanese oaks?"

"They're not in season either."

"Things have changed around here a bit, haven't they? I'm sure that wasn't a Starbucks."

"Yes, it's gotten a bit chic, hasn't it?"

This is the lane of cherry trees.

Every year in mid-April, this area is crowded with people who've come to drink and eat under the blossoms.

When the cherry trees are in bloom, we don't need to go looking for food.

We can eat and drink people's leftovers, and with the groundsheets they leave behind, we get brand-new roofs and walls for our huts, replacing tarps that have crumpled and begun to leak over the past year.

Today is Monday; the zoo is closed.

I never took my children to Ueno Zoo.

I came to work in Tokyo at the end of 1963. Yoko was five then, and Kōichi was just three.

The pandas came to Ueno Zoo nine years later. The kids were both in middle school by then, past the age when they would want to go to the zoo.

I didn't take them to the zoo, nor to the amusement park, the seaside, the mountains; I never went to their beginning-of-year ceremonies or graduations or to a parents' open day or to a sports day, not even once.

I went back only twice a year, in summer and in winter, to my village in Fukushima, where my parents, my brothers and sisters, and my wife and children waited for me.

One year when I was able to return a few days before the Bon holidays, there was a festival or something, and I took my children to Haramachi for a day out.

Haramachi was only one station from Kashima, but it was the height of summer and it was hot on the train, making me lethargic. I was hit by drowsiness, the children's excited voices and my halfhearted responses felt indistinct, as if I were in a fog, while the train cut across the endless landscapes of sky, mountains, farmlands, and rice fields, passing through the tunnel before accelerating. I saw my children's hands, outstretched like geckos', and their foreheads and lips glued to the window, beyond which there was only blue and green. The tang of their sweat filled my nose, and for just a few moments I let my head drop.

When we got off at Haramachi, the ticket inspector told us that we might be able to take a helicopter ride in Hibarigahara, so I set off down the Hamakaidō Road with Yoko's hand in my right and Kōichi's in my left.

Kōichi, who saw me too rarely to even miss me and never tried to pull anything or get his way, squeezed my hand. "Daddy, I want to go on the helicopter." I can see his face clearly now in my mind, wanting to say something, opening and closing his mouth several times before he finally spoke and, in the end, turning bright red as if in anger. But I had no money. The helicopter ride cost about three thousand yen at that time, or over thirty thousand in today's money. . . . It was too much.

Instead I bought them each a Matsunaga ice cream, which cost fifteen yen then. Yoko brightened up immediately, but Kōichi turned his back to me and began to cry, his body shaking with sobs as he watched the helicopter take off, full of boys with wealthy parents.

He pawed at his tears with his fists.

That day the sky was as blue as a strip of cloth. I wanted to give him that helicopter ride, but I couldn't afford it, and so I didn't—I still regret it. And ten years later, on that awful day, that regret again stabbed my heart, it is still with me now, it never leaves—

They never move, the red strokes that spell the words UENO ZOO like scratches on an arm, nor do the fingers of the children wearing red, blue, and yellow, arms raised over the fence, on the sign for the children's amusement park.

Trembling like a solitary reed, I want to talk as much as I can, but I don't know how to go about it. I fumble for a way out, I want to see one so badly, but the darkness does not fall nor does the light shine in. It's over, but it never ends . . . this constant anguish, sorrow, grief—

A gust of wind rustled through the trees, shaking the leaves and sending drops of water falling, though the rain seemed to have stopped.

At Sakuragitei, the little red-and-white lanterns swayed in the wind and a woman in a red apron stood on a stepladder, brushing off the faded pink awning, which read, in white letters, PANDA CAKES.

Seated on the wooden bench in front of the restaurant were two old ladies. The one on the left had a white cardigan over her shoulders.

"I brought some pictures with me. Shall we have a look?" Rummaging in her yellow bag, she pulled out a small album and opened it to a group photograph, thirty older men and women standing in three neat rows.

The woman on the right, wearing a black cardigan rather larger than her friend's white one, reached for a pair of reading glasses from her shoulder bag, then began to trace her finger over the photo in big, slow circles like an uncoiled spring.

"This woman here, this is Mr. Yamazaki's wife, isn't it? And there he is, too."

"They always did come as a pair. Practically inseparable."

"And this fellow, he was the head of the student association. . . ."

"Shimizu."

"And oh, that's Tomo!"

"Her smile always did have a hint of sadness to it."

"And here you are, my dear. Look at you, you look just like a movie star."

"Oh, stop it."

The two old women were sitting so close that their shadows had become one. A pigeon marched around their shadow as if seeking something.

Above their heads two crows screeched a shrill warning at each other.

"Next to Takeuchi here, that's Mr. Yamamoto, isn't it? He runs an antiques shop. And that's Sonoda Shoko. . . ."

"No, that's Yumi."

"Oh, yes, Yumi. You saw her at Yuko's wake, didn't you?"

"All these decades later, and we knew each other right away."

"And that's what's-his-name from the office. . . ."

"Mr. Iiyama."

"Yes, Iiyama."

"And next to him is . . ."

"Oh, that's . . . Hiromi, isn't it?"

"Yes, yes, yes, Hiromi."

"And that's Mucchan."

"She hasn't aged a bit, you know."

"And then there's Ms. Shinohara."

"Wearing a kimono as always."

"Isn't she lovely?"

"That's Fumi, and Take, and Chii, and that's Ms. Kurata—the only one who was in a different class."

"Oh, I never realized that."

"She lived in Kawasaki, but there was a prowler in her neighborhood that caused her a lot of trouble. Once, in a hotel at Echigo-Yuzawa, when everyone else was asleep, this man stayed up drinking tea and talking, although everyone had gone to bed. He just wouldn't stop talking."

"Oh, what a hassle."

"It was. He was somebody's husband, this man who

went prowling about. She found him in her garden one time."

"How frightening. And with him living in the neighborhood, she couldn't exactly call the police, I suppose."

I never carried any photos with me, but I was always surrounded by people, places, and times gone by. And as I retreated into the future, the only thing I could ever see was the past.

It was nothing as sweet as nostalgia or a longing for bygone days, just a constant absence from the present, an anger toward the future. I was always lost at a point in the past that would never go anywhere now that it had gone, but has time ended? Has it just stopped? Will it someday rewind and start again? Or will I be shut out from time for eternity? I don't know, I don't know, I don't know.

When I lived with my family, we took no photos together.

By the time I was old enough to understand the world around me, the war had begun, and food shortages meant my stomach was always empty.

And in the shadow of my having been born seven or eight years too late, the war ended without me going off to fight.

There were boys in my village who volunteered at seventeen and became soldiers, and there were boys who, in an effort to flunk their physical examination for enrollment, drank soy sauce or pretended their eyes or ears were bad.

I was twelve when the war ended.

There was no time for abjection, for feeling sad that we lost the war—all I could think of was eating or feeding others. It was difficult enough to feed one child, and I had seven brothers and sisters younger than me. There were no TEPCO nuclear plants or Tohoku Electric Power plants along the coast at that time, no Hitachi or Del Monte factories. Big farmers could feed themselves easily, but the few paddies my family had were insignificant at best, so as soon as I graduated from elementary school, I left home to work at Onahama Port in Iwaki, lodgings provided.

I say lodgings were provided, but instead of in a dormitory or apartment we slept in a large fishing boat.

Between April and September, we fished for skipjack; September to November we caught Pacific saury, mackerel, sardines, tuna, and flounder.

The problem with life on a boat was lice. Every time I changed clothes, I could see the lice brushing off—they were in the very stitching—and when I got the slightest bit warm, I could feel them creeping around on my back—quite the nuisance.

I lasted two years in Onahama.

My father had started gathering surf clams on Kitamigita Beach, so I decided to go back and help him.

We would go out to sea in a little wooden boat, dragging a metal harrow along the bottom, pulling up the ropes by hand as we had no wire, our feet pushing against the boat—pull, push—my father and I pulling up surf clams day after day.

Everyone else in our village and every other village harvested surf clams, keeping at it without giving the clams time to reproduce, so within four or five years there were none left.

The year that my son, Kōichi, was born, my uncle pulled some strings to get me a job. He himself had left Yazawa for Hokkaido to find work, and now I headed off to harvest kelp in a fishing village called Hamanaka, near Kiritappu in Hokkaido.

During my holidays in May, I planted rice, leaving fertilizing and weeding until Nomaoi, the local horse-racing festival that had been held since time immemorial. In the village of Sōma, everything from work in the fields to house repairs to even the repayment of debts is put off "until Nomaoi," like putting things on the never-never, such a milestone is the Nomaoi festival in our calendar.

Nomaoi is held on the twenty-third, twenty-fourth, and twenty-fifth days of July.

First is the night festival. The leader sets off from Naka-mura Shrine in Sōma and is joined by another rider at Kitago Honjin. Then horseback warriors from Uta and Kita townships cross and join, followed by warriors from many other townships, who join at Ota Shrine and at Odaka Shrine.

The second day marks the main festival. At the sound of a conch-shell horn and war drums, the five hundred horsemen advance at once, and the Kacchu Keiba race and flag competition commence at Hibarigahara.

The third day is the Nomagake. At Odaka Shrine, men clad in white, sporting white headbands, capture wild horses with their bare hands and offer them as part of a religious ritual. Because it costs so much to rent a horse and put together a set of samurai armor, the poor have almost nothing to do with the festival, but when I was five or six, I went to the deputy general's house with my father and he put me on his shoulders so I could see the preparations for the horse show.

"They'll set off at twelve thirty."

"Twelve thirty on the dot. I'll return immediately and let everyone know."

"Thank you. Could you please tell Kitago Temple to prepare?"

"I will. Sir, I beg your pardon for the unpleasantness involving the horses at Utago Honjin. I shall return immediately."

"Thank you again. Take care on the road."

Sōma nagareyama, na-e, na-e, ssai!
Naraitakya gosare, na-e, e-ssai!
Gogatsu no saru, na-e, na-e, ssai!
Are sa o Nomaoi, na-e, e-ssai!

The samurai straddled their horses and headed off down the footpaths between the lush rice fields—it was fun to see all their different flags waving in the breeze. "Oh, that one's got a centipede on it!" "Look at the snakes on that one!" "That flag's got a horse rearing up on it!" I shouted at my dad from his shoulders, pointing up at the flags.

When I left home to go work in Hokkaido, it took me two nights on the train to get there. I rode the Jōban Line from Kashima to Sendai, then the Tōhoku Main Line to Aomori. From there I took the ferry to Hakodate, arriving in the morning.

In Hakodate I boarded the Hakodate Main Line, needing to cross the Tokachi Mountains and Karikachi Pass, but even with two engines the train could barely muster the steam needed to move forward. We alighted with our bags, and still the train struggled to gather enough speed to overtake us on the platform.

This was the same year as the 9.5-magnitude earthquake in Chile. I remember that eleven people died in Kiritappu from the ensuing tsunami. I was surprised to see household items like blankets hanging from electric poles, and I asked my uncle, who had been living in Hamanaka for a while, "Did the water really get that high? Really?"

"It did. They say it was about twenty feet. And with the 1952 Tokachi-Oki earthquake, a big tsunami came, cutting

Kiritappu off from the mainland and turning it into an island. Originally it had been connected by a bridge, but the tsunami washed the bridge away," he explained. We stood by the seafront, our bodies stiff in the cold.

The sea was covered with kelp. It could get to be over fifty feet long, so we dragged a rod behind the boat to gather it to us, then pulled it in by hand. When we returned to port, the kelp was unloaded onto horse-drawn carts, then spread out to dry on the beach until the whole beach was black with kelp.

I did this for two months, then returned home in October to harvest rice. This pattern continued for three years.

I spoke with my father, whose bones had started aching and who wasn't long for agricultural work, about how my brothers were hoping to go away for school and how Yoko and Kōichi would be needing more money soon. I decided to go to Tokyo to look for work.

The year before the Tokyo Olympics, on the cold morning of December 27, 1963, I left my house while it was still dark, went to Kashima Station, and caught the first Jōban Line train at 5:33. It was just past noon when I arrived at Ueno Station. I was embarrassed by my soot-streaked face, pitch-black from the smoke of the locomotive after all the tunnels we'd passed through, and I remember that my face was reflected over and over in the windows of the train as I walked along the platform, pulling the brim of my hat down, then up again.

I got a room in a dormitory in Taishidō, Setagaya. The dorm was a prefab, and each man had a six-mat room with a shared toilet and bath. In the mornings and evenings, those of my colleagues who could cook made rice, miso soup, and some simple side dishes, which they shared with me. Because of the heavy labor we had to do, if we didn't eat two bowls of rice a day, our bodies would simply have stopped functioning.

Nothing so useful as canned meals existed then, and even if they had, I wouldn't have had the money to buy them, so after breakfast I would fill a bowl with rice, put a plate on top, tie it up in a cloth, and take a train to the site. We had an hour's break, so I would buy croquettes or a deep-fried cutlet from the shops near the site to eat with my rice.

Our job was constructing athletics facilities—the track and baseball fields and the tennis and volleyball courts to be used in the Tokyo Olympics. Although this was construction work, I never saw any heavy equipment like bulldozers or diggers, and we laborers down from the countryside wouldn't have been able to operate those machines anyway, so everything was done by human force: we dug the earth with picks and shovels and carried the soil away in hand-carts. Many of us were from farming families in Tōhoku. Everyone joked about how construction was just like plowing the fields. At five when we put our work aside, we'd go for a drink together, but for better or worse I couldn't hold my liquor. Nevertheless, so many times when someone said, "C'mon, tonight's on me!" I couldn't say no, and I would try to go along with things out of politeness. Eventually people stopped asking me out, as one glass of beer was my limit.

My daily wage of a thousand yen was three or four times what I could get working the same hours back home. Overtime was paid at time and a quarter, so I worked late every night with pleasure and went out to work on Sundays and holidays, too.

Pay was totaled on the fifteenth. Every month I sent home twenty thousand yen or thereabouts. This was about the same as a teacher's monthly earnings at the time, and in today's money this would be about two hundred thousand yen, I think.

"Work's all dried up these days," said the homeless man, snapping off a maple branch. His jean jacket reminded me of something. The white splotch on the back, perhaps caused by spilled bleach, was shaped a lot like Hokkaido, which made it all the more certain—that was my jacket. I'd found it at a trash-collection point in Hirokoji on textile-waste day, and I treasured it on those chilly days in early spring. I'd left it hanging from the ceiling of my tent, but obviously someone must've taken it—after I disappeared.

"With the economy this bad, they treat you like shit wherever you go—big companies, small companies, doesn't matter," said an old woman with white hair like a bird's nest, her layered, tattered skirts fluttering. She lit up a Hi-Lite cigarette and took a drag.

I know this face . . . those smooth cheeks, so out of place on her aged face . . . I know them. Good morning, she'd greet me sometimes. We must've stood and chatted before. . . .

"The places with thirty or forty employees are the worst off. They're the most unprepared."

"The other day I was on the Odakyū Line."

"Goes to some pretty trendy places, doesn't it?"

"That's where Shige used to live, before he died."

"Shige's dead?"

"Yeah, he died. They found him gone cold in his tent."

"Well, I gotta say, he was pretty old."

The woman's eyes sank suddenly, glazed. I wanted to comfort her, but I could not put my hand on her shoulder or give her my condolences.

I knew Shige. He was an intellectual. He was always reading discarded newspapers, magazines, and books. I think he must have once had a job where he used his head.

One day someone threw a kitten into his tent, and he used the money he made selling cans to get it neutered. He named it Emile and doted on him. When we were evicted from the park, he'd put Emile in his handcart, and when it rained, he'd shelter him with his umbrella.

And Shige's the one who told me about the hall with the face of the Buddha built by a priest from Kan'ei-ji Temple, on the hill on the other side of the "time bell," which had been built to mark time for the people of Edo at five in the morning and evening and at noon.

"The Giant Buddha lost its head four times, three times in earthquakes and once in a fire, which really is too tragic. The first time it fell off was in 1647, and since it would have been a shame to leave it that way, the monks went all around Edo one day asking for alms to fund the repairs. Nobody gave them a thing. But as the sun was beginning to set on their way home, a beggar approached and put some small change in their alms bowl. And with that it's said that the donations started coming in and the monks were able to put together the Giant Buddha, which was almost twenty-three feet high. Almost two hundred years later, the head fell off again due to a fire, and though they put it back exactly as it had been, ten years later in another earthquake it fell off again and had to be repaired again. It made it through the Battle of Ueno in 1868 unharmed, but in the 1923 Great Kantō Earthquake it was completely destroyed."

He was a special person. He could speak at length on any subject, like a teacher, and possibly he really might've been a teacher before he became homeless.

On that particular day, I had been telling Shige about a

radio tower. It was so famous in Hamadōri, the area that I came from, that it was almost synonymous with Haramachi, and it was a symbol of the town until it was demolished in 1982. Its construction was completed in 1921, and two years later it sent the telegraph that informed the entire world of the 1923 Great Kantō Earthquake: "Major earthquake noon today in Yokohama, followed by major fire, whole city in flames, unknown number dead, all transport and communication facilities destroyed."

Then Shige told me that though the surrounding area had been set ablaze, Ueno Park had not burned, largely due to the water in Shinobazu Pond. The Matsuzakaya Department Store opposite the park was completely destroyed. Local residents, and even people from as far as Nihonbashi and Kyōbashi, flooded into the park, seeking refuge from the flames. Some had brought everything they owned in large handcarts, hoping to return to their families in the countryside. So many flooded in that they blocked the roads around the station as well as the tracks, so no trains could move. The base of the statue of Takamori Saigō was plastered with notes from those seeking missing friends and family members, of which there were many. Emperor Hirohito, then the imperial prince, came in military uniform to inspect the park. He saw how incredibly important this park, crowded with victims, was in times of disaster. In January 1924, the reigning emperor presented the park to the city as a New Year's gift. Thus it has the official name of Ueno Imperial Gift Park.

As Shige spoke, he looked tenderly at Emile, who lay on his side in the grass with both eyes closed, the end of his long tail twitching.

I never told Shige that I had once seen Emperor Hirohito up close.

On August 5, 1947, at 3:35 P.M., the royal train stopped at Haramachi Station. The emperor disembarked and spent seven minutes at the station.

I had just returned home from a stint away, working at the harbor in Konahama.

The sky was oppressively blue. The calls of the brown cicadas shook Honjinyama itself, and the Mingming cicadas chirped constantly, as if in competition. The liquid sunshine quivered and licked at us, and the green leaves and white shirts on people's backs were all so bright that I struggled to keep my eyes open, but as one of the twenty-five thousand people waiting in front of the station for the emperor, I kept my hat on my head and stayed perfectly still.

At the moment that the emperor, dressed in a suit, descended from the royal train and touched his hand to the brim of his fedora in greeting, we cried out, "Long live the emperor! Banzai!" as if it were being wrung out of us, and we raised our arms in the air, a wave of banzai welling up.

"Can you believe that, that Shige's dead?"

"The ash from your cigarette almost never falls."

"When you've been smoking for eighty-five years, you get pretty good at it."

"You started smoking when you were a baby, did you?"

"Shige's dead!"

"Did you do it with him?"

"Go hang yourself!"

"What are you getting so worked up for, you filthy old bag?"

"You bastard! I'll have your fucking heart right out of your chest!"

"Oh, you're scarier than an old hag from San'ya. . . . Look at that fucking tick!" The old homeless man slapped at his own shin.

"That's an ant, you idiot."

The old woman's gaze fell to her legs. She looked at the leather shoe on her left foot, then the running shoe on her right foot, and noticed that the laces were untied but did not move to retie them.

"Oh, quit fidgeting around and sit down. Sit!"

"I'd sit if there were seats anywhere."

"Just sit down."

The old man sat down on the concrete wall surrounding the tree and took a piece of paper out of his pocket.

"This might get me about five thousand yen. If I win, you can have half."

The woman leaned over and read out the words on the betting slip.

"'Evening session, Thirty-fifth Running of the Emperor's Cup, eleventh race, trifecta, number one, number twelve, number three, five hundred yen; first: number one, Oerai-jin, jockey Kimura Ken; second: number twelve, Miracle Legend, jockey Uchida Hiroyuki; third: number three, Tosengoraiasu, jockey Hashimoto Naoya.'"

She dropped her cigarette, crushing it under her leather shoe, yet smoke still rose from the butt. A line of ants marched past her feet, climbing up a tree one by one, but ants don't make their homes in trees. In Ueno Park—this imperial gift—each tree has a round plastic tag attached to its trunk, like a locker key does. This tree was labeled Green A620—I try now to remember the feeling of its smooth, dry bark, the feeling of ants crawling across my skin, but ants don't make their homes in trees. The ants marched back down the tree. They went down the asphalt slope speckled with pigeon droppings and headed toward a group of huts that were surrounded by metal panels with pictures of trees on them, hidden by a blue tarp with a design of white clouds rigged up over the metal paneling.

A radio in one of the huts was tuned in to a debate in the National Diet.

> *"The government is fully aware that many citizens
> have complex feelings regarding the accident in March
> last year, and we know that we must act responsibly
> on this issue dividing the nation, which is why the
> government intends to provide a full explanation
> in due time."*
>
> *"Mr. Yasunori Saito!"*

"Thank you, Mr. Speaker. The current security protocols are based on the myth that nuclear power is completely safe, and the idea of restarting the nuclear power stations while working under these protocols provokes anger in all who can see the inherent contradictions of the situation. Many voices of protest are rising in opposition to this absurdity. I call on the prime minister now to reflect on the situation and . . ."

I heard the sound of a lawn mower somewhere nearby.

The smell of freshly cut grass hit me.

Then the smell of someone making instant ramen in their tent.

A sparrow startled at something and suddenly flew off, like a handful of beans scattered at Setsubun to cast out evil.

The hydrangeas were in bloom. The lighter blossom surrounding the smaller, darker center resembled a demon's face.

Things like that always made me feel lonely when I was alive.

Now noises, colors, and smells are all mixed up, gradually fading away, shrinking; I feel if I put out my finger to touch it, everything will disappear, but I have no fingers to touch with. I can no longer touch, not even one hand to the other in prayer.

If I don't exist, I can't disappear either.

"Mr. Prime Minister."

"I am of course aware of the various opinion polls going around. But since its formation in September last year, this government considers that, for victims of this disaster, the most important things are reconstruction, battling the consequences of the nuclear accident, and the revival of the Japanese economy. These are our priorities, and I am determined to take all measures necessary to provide genuine aid to victims of the disaster."

Raindrops suddenly began to fall, wetting the roofs of the huts. They fell regularly, like the weight of life or of time. On nights when it rained, I couldn't stop myself from listening to the sound, which kept me from sleeping. Insomnia, then eternal sleep—held apart from one by death and the other by life, brought closer to one by life and the other by death, and the rain, the rain, the rain, the rain.

It rained on the day that my only son died.

———·———

TODAY AT FOUR FIFTEEN P.M., THE CROWN PRINCESS
GAVE BIRTH TO A SON AT THE IMPERIAL HOSPITAL.
MOTHER AND CHILD ARE DOING WELL.

It was the twenty-third of February, 1960. I heard the announcer read the news exultantly over the radio.

Not long after, they broadcast the sounds of the cheering crowds gathered in front of Nijubashi Bridge and the Tōgū Palace, red-and-white lanterns in their hands, beating drums, singing the national anthem, and chanting, "Long live the emperor!"

The fireworks continued to explode outside, twenty or thirty times, I think, and then they started going off over by Kashima Town Hall, boom, boom, boom. . . .

Setsuko had gone into labor the morning of the day before.

It was a horrible labor, unlike the birth of our daughter, Yoko, two years before. Setsuko was in agony for nearly an entire day, and my mother told her over and over again in our dialect, "It happens, honey, everything's gonna be fine, the baby will be here before night falls," but her voice began to tremble and the anxiety became apparent in her eyes. At the end of the second day, Setsuko was writhing in pain, her crimson face framing gritted teeth. I went to her parents' house in the same village for advice, and they told me to go and fetch Imano Toshi, a reputable midwife in Kashima.

I went back to my parents' house to tell them I was going to go fetch a midwife. My mother said nothing; my father's face was grave. On the radio, a different announcer revealed that the imperial prince had just met his son for the first time. "Congratulations to His Majesty the Crown Prince and to Her Majesty the Crown Princess. The people of this nation rejoice at the sight of the young prince, their voices crying passionately for his long life. We give our sincere congratulations." I saw in the dim reflection of the windowpane in the darkened room that I was the only one crying. I knew that we did not have enough to pay the midwife and that there was no time to borrow the money, not that anyone would have lent it anyway. I swallowed hard, my mouth flooded again with saliva, and the noise of the radio grew faint. I swallowed again and no longer heard even the silence.

My mother and father vanished from my sight; I ran outside. But as I ran, I thought about money. The phrase repeated in my mind: I don't have a single sen, I don't have a single sen.

We were at our very poorest when Kōichi was born. I helped my dad out by gathering clams in Kitamigita Bay, but the money instantly went to pay off our outstanding debts with the moneylender, the hardware store, the rice and sake merchants, and after that there was nothing left.

To keep us all fed, my mother and Setsuko would go out every day from spring to autumn, except when it was raining, planting rice, potatoes, pumpkins, and greens to harvest and bring home.

And in the winter, my mother and Setsuko would knit sweaters for everyone in the family. We could afford only cheap yarn and thread, so the sweaters quickly developed holes, but the women would repair them neatly. I liked watching the movement of their hands as they worked: my youngest sister, Michiko, holding the unraveled yarn stretched between her hands as my mother and Setsuko took it and wound it into balls. Michiko would try to badger them into singing something, which Setsuko never would do, being a shy woman of few words, but my mother would sing a lullaby in dialect. When Michiko asked her where she had learned it, she said warmly, "I learned that one when I went off to be a nanny for a sake merchant. I must've been seven or eight." When I realized that the words of the song were about how looking after children isn't as easy as you might think, my eyes stung and I felt a lump in my throat.

Bill collectors came to our door year-round.

We'd send my youngest brothers, still just kids, to tell them nobody was in, but the collectors didn't buy that.

"Now, don't lie to me, boys. Where'd they go? When're they coming back?"

"They said they didn't know when they were coming back," my brother said, snot dripping from his nose.

"Are you sure your mama's not home? I just want a word with her."

My brother began to cry. "Mama's gone to Haramachi. She's not home."

"You don't say. Well, tell 'em I'll be back," the collector grumbled as he left.

I was relieved that he left, of course, but at the same time I thought what a thing of sin poverty was, that there could be nothing more sinful than forcing a small child to lie. The wages of that sin were poverty, a wage that one could not endure, leading one to sin again, and as long as one could not pull oneself out of poverty, the cycle would repeat until death.

These attacks and retreats by bill collectors were interrupted only during the fifteen days when all the houses were decorated with pine branches for the New Year. On New Year's Eve, my family, all ten of us, would go to Shoen-ji Temple in Kashima to hear the bell ring in the New Year, and the next day we would give very meager envelopes of money to my brothers and sisters before playing some traditional games. Kite-flying, badminton, cards, pin the tail on the donkey . . .

February was always the most difficult time of the year.

Ten days before Kōichi was born, some officials from the tax office trampled through our house, attaching red slips of paper to almost everything. They didn't touch the rice cooker or the table, of course, but they marked the chest of drawers, the radio, and the clock.

"You're doing us a favor, you know, taking all this old

shit away," my father spat, drunk on cheap hooch. I felt pathetic waking up and eating meals in a house full of repossession notices.

I can't remember if that day, the day Kōichi was born, was before or after they took everything away.

What I do remember is how cold it was, how the snow danced in the wind as I ran, and how I pressed my face close to the nameplate on the house to make sure it really said IMANO before knocking on the door. I remember that I did not ask how much it would cost and that she didn't say anything about money either; I remember the white cap that she put on when she entered our house, her white apron, the trumpet-shaped black stethoscope she put to Setsuko's big belly; I remember listening to the radio in the living room while I waited, hearing a cry, and then her voice as she told me, "It's a boy, congratulations. And born the same day as the prince—what a blessing."

I leaned to look at the futon and saw Setsuko cradling a baby to her chest. He had already begun to nurse.

But the first thing I saw was not the baby, it was Setsuko's arm, bent like a sickle, muscles defined and skin tanned from working in the fields.

The midwife, who had spoken in standard Japanese all

this time, repeated her congratulations in our dialect, and Setsuko laughed, her whole body shaking with laughter, which made her grimace with pain. She let go of the baby and put her hands to her face, which was covered with sweat despite the cold, and then smiled again.

Her smile broke the tension, and I dared then to look at the baby's face.

I was a father looking down at his son for the first time, and yet I felt like a baby looking up at his mother's face. Suddenly I wanted to cry.

As he was born on the same day as the crown prince's first son, I decided that we would call him Kōichi, borrowing the first character of the prince's name for the first of his own.

"The smell must be awful, though."

"Well, I keep it in the entrance hall."

"That doesn't mean it doesn't smell."

"True. But I'm used to it now. I've almost forgotten it's there."

The woman, in her mid-thirties, held a soda bottle in

one hand and the leashes for three toy poodles in the other as she spoke to a slightly plump woman around the same age. The white dog had a red lead, the gray one a pink lead, and the brown one a blue lead.

"It must be expensive to feed three dogs," said the plump woman. "What do you give them?"

"I cook up a mix of rice and chicken tenders or lean beef in a big pot, and when they get hungry, I heat some up and give it to them, but they can get sick if they don't get enough vegetables, so I throw in some radish or carrot or some lettuce. Anyway, I give them a lot of greens."

"I swear, they eat better than people."

"Honestly. I mean, all I need is a bread roll."

"Do bread rolls still exist? Like the kind you get in a cafeteria?"

"I found some in a little bakery on a back street."

The clip-clop of their shoes rang out. When one of them stepped on a fallen leaf, there was a rustling sound, too. I can no longer hear sounds or voices with my ears. But I feel like I'm listening closely. I can't watch people anymore either. But I feel like I'm watching intently. And I can't speak about what I hear or see anymore. But I can talk to people. The people in my memories, whether they're alive or dead—

"Almost time for the morning-glory market, isn't it?"

"It's Friday and Saturday the week after next."

"Kototoi Street is going to be absolutely wild."

"I heard there's going to be about a hundred stalls."

A group of elderly people in baseball caps and straw hats gather around an art student, sitting on a little stool on the pavement painting a watercolor of a tree. They all have their hands stuck in their pockets or linked behind their backs or their arms folded over their chests.

Nobody is carrying an umbrella. The pavement is dry.

Today is going to be one of those days when it rains on and off.

Today . . .

One day . . .

It was raining that day. I put my head down to keep the cold rain off my face, looking down as the water bounced off the pavement around my wet shoes like oil popping in a frying pan, the rain beating down on me, my shoulders hunched, walking in the rain.

"All the girls are going to be wearing summer kimonos with morning-glory patterns."

"Girls these days don't wear kimonos."

"But they do! It's such a pretty sight."

"Every year I buy two plants, and I think they're going to bloom, but then I have to practically convince them to do it. Morning glories are from much farther south, and you have to put them somewhere very sunny, but in the daytime their leaves start drooping like a dog's ears, so you have to give them some rainwater or the leftover water from washing rice. Then, during the summer, when the blooms start to fade, I pinch them off, so when the plant blooms for the last time in September, it will give me seeds for the next year."

A cyclist stopped by the side of the road.

They stopped right in front of the Statue of Times Forgotten, the memorial to the victims of the firebombing of Tokyo, so perhaps it was someone who'd lost family then.

One night while we were queuing to buy tickets from a scalper, Shige told me about it.

"The American firebombing of Tokyo began at eight minutes past midnight on the tenth of March, 1945. Over three hundred B-29s flying at low altitude dropped seventeen hundred incendiary bombs on the most densely populated, working-class part of the city. A fierce north wind was blowing that night, which soon turned the fire into a tsunami of flames, engulfing the streets. The highest death toll was reportedly at Kototoi Bridge, where people living on either side of the river had assumed that safety lay across the water. People ran with children in their arms or on their backs; they escaped on bicycles, pushed carts full of their most treasured possessions or elderly family members. . . . Then the flames from the Asakusa side of the river started to leap, and those who were on fire tried to cross to the other side. By morning the bridge was covered with burned bodies. Seven thousand people were temporarily buried in Sumida Park, on both sides of the river, and seventy-eight hundred were brought to Ueno Park and buried here. In just two hours that night, over a hundred thousand people lost their lives, but there's not a single public monument to them anywhere in the city, nothing like the peace parks in Hiroshima and Nagasaki."

Next to the bicycle in front of the Statue of Times Forgotten, a skinny man in his sixties bobbed down, checking his reflection in the bike's mirror as he shaved. Using a large pair of gardening shears, he scraped at his beard. He looked trim in his black T-shirt and white trousers, but the tent, saucepan, umbrella, and flip-flops piled onto the bike's luggage rack, in addition to the wet clothes and towel pinned to the basket, suggested that this man was homeless after all. Was he shaving because he'd found some work as a day laborer? At his age, engineering or construction work was out of the question, but one could possibly earn a thousand yen a day cleaning office buildings on Saturdays, mopping the hallways and lobbies from the first floor to the tenth, waxing them once dry.

The Statue of Times Forgotten depicts a woman carrying a baby boy in her right arm while her left hand rests on the shoulder of a little girl. The little girl is looking up and pointing at the sky to the right, and the baby looks up to the right, too, but the mother faces straight ahead.

As we waited in line for the ticket office to open, Shige told me more about the firebombing of Tokyo. Unlike when he'd told me about other places in Ueno Park, like the Great Buddha or the Shimizu Kannon Temple, now he spoke as if he were desperately trying to chase away the fear and sadness he was grappling with, and I wondered if he, as a survivor of the bombardment, had come upon the corpse of someone from his own family here. Perhaps he had made his life here in the park, in a tent, as a result. But it was winter; I was cold, and my lips were so dry that I could barely speak, and I didn't want to attempt to find out whether my guess about Shige was right.

"The tenth of March was Armed Forces Day, and the next day was a Sunday, so many of the children who had been sent away from their homes to stay in the countryside, sleeping in temples or hotels, had come back to the city on the ninth for the holiday weekend. Many of the bodies found in Ueno Park were the burned, blackened corpses of parents and children, still clinging to one another."

Each time I saw the Statue of Times Forgotten, I felt like I was being forced to face those times gone by. Yoko and Kōichi were only two years apart, so there must've been a time when they looked just like this. I was never home, because I was away working, so I didn't take any pictures of the children. I never had my own camera either.

I have only one picture of Kōichi, a tiny photo of him from his student card when he was at technical school learning to be a radiographer. When we had it enlarged for his funeral, his face was blurry, as if he were behind frosted glass.

Like it was someone else completely.

But it really was Kōichi that died.

After the Tokyo Olympics ended, the wave of urbanization reached the Tōhoku region and Hokkaido, bringing with it public works projects such as building new highways, railways, parks, and riverbank protection structures, as well as the construction of schools, hospitals, libraries, and other public facilities. When Tanikawa Athletics Co. Ltd., the company I worked for, opened up a branch office in Sendai, I was transferred there to work on site at construction projects, building baseball stadiums, tennis courts, and other athletic facilities.

That day it had been raining since I awoke. I was digging out the future site of Sukagawa City Hall's tennis court with a pickax.

When I returned to my room that night, I had a call from work. "Mr. Mori, your wife called to tell you that your son is dead," they said.

Just a few days earlier, Setsuko had called to say that Kōichi had passed the national radiology exam, so I assumed there must've been a mistake, but when I called home, she told me that Kōichi had been found dead at the apartment where he lodged, on his futon as if he were sleeping, and that the police were carrying out an autopsy because they suspected that his death might be unnatural.

It was raining.

Yoko's husband, who was from Sendai, picked up Setsuko first at the house in Yazawa, then drove to Sukagawa to get me.

It was raining.

What we talked about on the ride, or whether we talked at all, I cannot remember.

It was morning by the time we got to Tokyo.

It was raining.

At the morgue Kōichi's naked body was covered with a white sheet, and we were told that an autopsy was required to be carried out by the medical examiner.

When we left the morgue, it was raining.

Setsuko and I went to the apartment where Kōichi had lived for three years and stayed there. We lay on the futon, where he had died, until the morning.

What we talked about, or whether we talked at all, I cannot remember.

The next day when we left the apartment, it was raining.

When we arrived at the morgue, Kōichi had been dressed in a cotton kimono and placed in a coffin. Yoko and her husband, who spent the night at a nearby inn, had apparently arranged everything with the undertaker.

At the very bottom of the medical examiner's report, he had marked "death from illness or natural causes," and at the top there was Kōichi's name and date of birth.

Mori Kōichi, born February 23, 1960—the voice of that radio announcer twenty-two years ago came back to me.

TODAY AT FOUR FIFTEEN P.M., THE CROWN PRINCESS GAVE BIRTH TO A SON AT THE IMPERIAL HOSPITAL. MOTHER AND CHILD ARE DOING WELL.

———

We placed his remains in the room where he was born.

With both hands I lifted the white cloth covering his face.

I hadn't looked at his face so carefully since he was a baby.

Then, too, I had knelt beside him and leaned over the same way—

He'd been autopsied, but his face was unharmed.

I looked at his face.

Arched eyebrows, a stubby nose, and thick lips—he looked like me.

I had been away from home constantly since he was born, and I'd seldom had the chance to walk beside him, so no one had ever had the chance to tell me that they could see a resemblance or that he looked just like me; nor were there any pictures of the two of us together, so I had never compared our faces in a photograph either.

Did Kōichi know that he looked like me?

Had Setsuko ever told him?

Yoko is the spitting image of her mother. Had she and her brother ever talked about which one took after their mother and which one took after their father?

I had no idea what my family had talked about for the twenty-odd years I'd been away from home.

While I'd been away, my brothers and sisters had all started their own families; my children had gotten through elementary, middle, and high school; Yoko had married; Kōichi had gone to Tokyo; my wife had been left alone at home with my elderly parents. And I'd had no choice but to keep working in Sendai, to pay for Kōichi's tuition and living expenses and to put food on my family's table.

I had lived this way since I was twelve and never felt

dissatisfied with it before—Kōichi had died in his sleep, and he still looked like he was just sleeping. I studied his face, that face that looked just like mine, and I could not help but think that my life had been pointless after all, that I had lived this life in vain.

Yoko cried as if her tears were being wrenched out of her.

Setsuko pressed her hand to her mouth. The gesture suggested she was trying to keep from sobbing or shrieking, but she did not cry.

I hadn't cried since I'd heard about Kōichi's death either.

I could not comprehend it.

I could not accept the sudden death of my only son at the age of twenty-one as reality.

My shock, my grief, my anger were all so great that crying felt inadequate.

The grandfather clock chimed, telling me that yet another hour had passed, but I couldn't make myself feel as though time were actually passing.

My mother, who was nearly eighty years old, brought her hands together in prayer, then pulled the white cloth back over her grandson's face. She said to me:

"You worked so hard to send us money all these years, and now when you ought to be able to take it easy . . . Well, you never did have any luck, did you? Better go to bed now—the funeral's tomorrow. Bath's already drawn." She stood up, tears spilling down her face.

I went to the bathroom and looked at myself in the chipped mirror, razor in hand.

It was disorienting to see the same face, as always, staring back at me.

Since Kōichi's naked body had been shown to me in the morgue, I had refused to call the corpse by his name, but the body lying in that room—it was Kōichi's body.

That was the face of my dead son.

Kōichi was dead.

And he would be tomorrow, too. From now on he would always be dead.

I began to tremble, from somewhere deep inside, and I could not quit, I could not find a way to calm down.

I went outside. The rain had stopped.

The air, washed by the rain, was serene, and the waves sounded closer than usual.

The full moon shone like a pearl in the night sky.

The moonlight made it look as if all the houses had sunk to the bottom of a lake.

The road stretched ahead, white.

It was the road that led to Migitahama.

A gust of wind and the petals from a wild cherry tree went dancing, white against the darkness, and I remembered then that the cherry trees here blossomed two or three weeks later than in Tokyo.

The waves roared.

I stood alone in the darkness.

Light does not illuminate.

It only looks for things to illuminate.

And I had never been found by the light.

I would always be in darkness—

I went back inside. Everyone was sleeping on the floor.

I changed into my pajamas, which were folded on top of my futon, laid my head on the pillow, and pulled the duvet over me.

I listened to the sounds of the house, and at some point I fell asleep. When I opened my eyes again, a faint light was filtering in through the gap in the curtains.

"You never did have any luck, did you?" My mother's

words had sunk into my heart like rain, and I clenched my fists under my duvet, turning my back to Setsuko.

As the chief mourner, I had to visit the home of the head of the neighborhood association.

The wind was warm and slightly stifling.

I saw the cherry trees rustle and petals fall.

The sky above me felt clear and endless as I walked.

Under this cloudless blue sky, another spring day had begun.

I'm trying, I thought.

Set me free from trying, I thought.

I'd been trying since I heard about Kōichi's death.

Until then I'd made an effort at work, but the effort I made now was to live.

It wasn't that I wanted to die; it was just that I was tired of trying.

A bird that was neither a swallow nor a wood pigeon nor a falcon, a bird with a pure white breast that I had never seen before, flew down from a branch of the cherry tree. Paying no mind to me despite the noise I made as I walked, it hopped around on the gravel like a new teacher walking back and forth in front of a blackboard with a stick of chalk in hand.

It disappeared from the corner of my eye, and when I turned around, it was no longer there.

The cherry petals continued to fall, and I wondered if perhaps the bird was Kōichi.

Time had slowed to a sluggish crawl. I walked faster, but each step plunged me deeper into the depths of stillness. If time could pass so slowly that its passage was imperceptible, then—is death where time stops and the self is left all alone in this space? Is death where space and the self are erased and only time continues? Where had Kōichi gone to? Had he really disappeared completely?

When I got home, the house was full of women in aprons bustling about, arranging flower wreaths and removing the sliding doors from their tracks. I heard the sound of multiple knives in the kitchen and realized that our neighbors and Setsuko's family must've come over to help, knives and chopping boards in hand.

I remembered the day that Setsuko and I were married in this house. She was twenty-one; I'd heard that she'd been married before, to a relative in Futaba, but that it hadn't worked out and she'd come back home. Setsuko and I had gone to the same elementary school, and we saw each other out walking or in the park, so there was no need for a formal introduction. Before we knew it, everything was decided, and one day I put on a black hakama with the family crest and went on foot with my family and friends to Setsuko. Her house was barely half a ri away, so by the time I brought her home, only an hour had passed. She wore a white kimono. No, it wasn't white, was it? The bride never wears white. Must've been black—but maybe her head-dress was white. . . .

Just when the sweet-and-sour smell of cooking had started to waft through the house, the chief priest from Shoen-ji Temple appeared on the veranda. He expressed his sympathy, saying that he would be the one carrying out the ceremony, then walked directly in from the veranda to the altar room.

The priest sat seiza in front of the altar, ringing the bowl-bell twice, as our relatives and the other faithful of our village also sat and clasped their hands.

Seeing the white cloth over Kōichi's face, the fire and smoke rising from the candles, and the funereal anise flowers that without my notice had taken the usual place of the small chrysanthemums on the altar, I was gripped by a panic that froze the blood in my veins.

"I, Ananda, heard the following from the Buddha, Shakyamuni. At one time, Shakyamuni was at the Jetavana in Shravasti, as many as twelve hundred and fifty people there assembled, and they were especially eminent monks, among them the elders Shariputra, Mahamaudgalyayana, Mahakashyapa. . . ."

I closed my eyes and took a breath, trying to focus on the Amida Sutra, but the palpitations were so strong I thought I might vomit, a mass of blood threatening to rise from the bottom of my throat at any moment.

Namu Amida Butsu, Namu Amida Butsu, Namu Amida Butsu . . . I heard my mother just next to my right ear chanting the nembutsu, and I tried to sing the hymns with the others. As breathless as if I had just run a mile I could not make a sound come out of my mouth for several minutes. My clasped hands felt cold and stiff.

"Without the strength of the Universal Vow
When could we leave this earthly world?
Thinking of the Buddha's benevolence
We keep our minds on Amida
And forget the eternal pain of this world

We wait for the Pure Land
With the strength of the Buddha
Let his mercy and goodness be known to the ages. . . ."

My father and mother, no matter how sick they were, always did their devotions each morning and evening.

It fell to my father to tell us about the trials of our ancestors. My mother listened while she knitted or did the mending, her face always showing the deep affection she held for these stories.

"Our family didn't always live in Sōma," he began. "About two hundred years ago, in 1803, in the Edo period, our ancestors suffered a hardship so bad it'd make your hair stand on end, and they came all this way here from Kaga-Etchū.

"Kaga-Etchū's in what we now call Toyama Prefecture, way down south, and there, in the Futsuka neighborhood of Nojiri village in Tonami district, there was a temple, Fugan-ji, whose head priest, Jokei, had four sons. Now, his second son, Korin, set up Jofuku-ji in Haramachi. His third son, Rinno, set up Shosai-ji in Sōma, and the fourth son, Hosen, opened Shofuku-ji in Futaba. That's why those three temples are called the Pathfinder Temples.

"Now, at the same time, Kakunen, the second son of

Entai, the superior of the Seien-ji, a temple in Aso village in Tonami, came to Sōma to set up a temple in this area, the Shoen-ji in Kashima.

"These men hoed and plowed the fields themselves, created salterns, grew rice to sell, and the money that they earned they used to bring ten families over from Kaga-Etchū every year.

"The hometown of our ancestors, seven generations ago, was Aso village, Tonami district, Toyama Prefecture, the same place Kakunen came from.

"Now, in those days there was no bus or train or nothing. They walked, from Echigo to Aizu, going through Nihonmatsu and Kawamata, before crossing the Yagisawa Pass and finally arriving in Sōma. They say it took damn near sixty days.

"Our ancestors had little more than the clothes on their backs, but thinking they'd need something to plant in this new land, they brought a green branch from a persimmon tree and stuck it in a fresh giant radish to keep it hydrated. They knew, even though persimmon trees take eight years to fruit while peach trees take only three, that persimmons'll see you through years of famine.

"That's why if you look in the garden of every True

Essence of the Pure Land follower, you'll find an ancient persimmon tree, and it's why we call them lotus persimmons or Toyama persimmons around here.

"Many of the villages in this area were settled by True Essence of the Pure Land followers. Our ancestors ended up with land that nobody else wanted. All the best farming land was already taken, so they wound up settling in the salt marshes near the sea or at the foot of the mountains where beasts ran wild.

"Sōma had a lot of temples from other sects like Shingon, Tendai, and Sōtō. People in Sōma always buried their dead, while Pure Land followers cremated them. In Sōma, when someone died, they placed six coins in the coffin to pay the dead's passage to the next world and dressed them in a white kimono with a walking stick and straw sandals; but Pure Land followers like us just dress the dead in white and nothing more, because when someone dies, they're returning to the Pure Land.

"Our people never worried whether a funeral would be on an auspicious day or an inauspicious one, because a funeral's something to celebrate. And we don't put a note on the house to warn people we're in mourning, 'cause death isn't an impurity, which is why we don't purify ourselves with salt after a funeral either.

"Sōma people have little Buddhist altars at home, but Pure Land followers have grand ones, and they're the heart of our homes.

"Sōma people put memorial tablets on their altars, but we put the dead's Buddhist name and death record.

"Houses in Sōma have a Shinto kamidana, a little altar devoted to Daikoku, the god of wealth, or Kokin, the god of the kitchen. And some of them hang amulets everywhere—the front door, the living room, the stables, the kitchen, even in the damn toilet! We don't do any of that.

"Sōma people celebrate just about every Shinto or Buddhist holiday, but we don't pay that kind of thing any mind. We don't put up New Year's decorations. And at Bon we don't put up special altars or light fires. How the hell is lighting a fire supposed to tell your ancestors that this is your house? You mean to tell me that someone who's reached enlightenment and been reborn as a Buddha needs a fire to tell them where to come back to? Load of horseshit if you ask me.

"I mean, at Bon they stab four sticks into cucumbers and eggplants and put them on their altars. The cucumber's supposed to be a horse, to bring your ancestors back quickly, and the eggplant's meant to be an ox, to bring them back slowly—hell, our ancestors weren't idiots! And they're not the kind of dead that only come home once a year anyway. No, when they die, they're reborn as Buddhas in the Pure Land that we'll all go back to eventually, and they watch over us three hundred sixty-five days a year, morning, noon, and night. Load of nonsense thinking they only come back during one week at Bon.

"It was written in the service book of the True Essence of the Pure Land sect that if you repeated the name of Amida Buddha, countless other Buddhas would surround you and bring happiness. These would be the dead, who had returned to the Pure Land and who would now protect us. Repeat it, over and over again: Namu Amida Butsu, be my protection both day and night.

"The guardian deity of the Sōma clan was an avatar of the bodhisattva Myōken, revered in the temples of Sōma-Nakamura, Haramachi-Ota, and Sōma-Odaka. In the old days, Pure Land followers didn't stop working in the fields even during the Nomaoi festival at the end of July. This really pissed off the 'natives,' who sometimes stole their tools to keep them from working during the festival.

"We called Sōma people 'the natives,' and they called us 'Kaga people' or ridiculed us for 'not knowing how to worship right.'

"Our ancestors suffered real bad, no doubt about it. Sure, the lord of the Sōma clan gave them land and promised them if they cleared the land and cultivated it, it would be theirs, but then he wouldn't give them the right to irrigate the land.

"I don't care how you cultivate land—you can't grow rice without water. Our ancestors struggled. They tried to talk to the natives, but the natives refused to sit down with them. Well, what could they do? Our ancestors got together and built their own reservoirs and channels.

"The natives had another nickname for us. They heard our ancestors chanting Namu Amida Butsu during their devotions morning and night and from a distance thought they were crying because they wanted to go back to Kaga. So the natives mocked the 'Kaga whiners.'

"Boy, did they suffer. But like Shinran said, 'The nembutsu is the only path without obstacle.' Our ancestors worked that barren land and were called names, but any pain or sorrow they felt didn't keep them from their path. Whatever happens to me, I just think about how bad they had it and I take it straight and keep on living."

The chime of the grandfather clock, which had been there since before I was born, rang out through the house.

The notion that Kōichi could not hear it seemed odd to me as I watched the movement of the brass pendulum. When the last chime had faded, the house became as silent as if it were underwater, and I could not help but think that he was listening to this silence, that Kōichi was listening.

A little before the clock struck six that evening, the faithful of our village and the neighboring one, Minami Migita, thronged our house with shikisho draped around their necks. They sat in front of the altar with the head priest from Shoen-ji and chanted, "Namu Amida Butsu."

After the wake three low tables for the post-wake meal were set up between the living room and the altar room, now one large room with the sliding doors removed.

My father told me what I needed to say as the chief mourner. I repeated his exact words to those who had come to pay their respects.

"Thank you all very much for coming to the wake for

my son, Kōichi, who died on the thirty-first of March in his apartment in Tokyo at the age of twenty-one. I would like to invite you to share this simple meal that we have prepared and to share your memories of Kōichi, too. The funeral will be held tomorrow at noon. Thank you for your support at this time."

I sat down with the chief priest, and Setsuko's relatives and our neighbors brought out vegetarian Buddhist dishes: burdock salad, vegetable stew, tofu salad, wild vegetable tempura, and pickles, as well as tableware. As the chief mourner, I walked around with a bottle of sake in both hands, filling up the glasses of those present.

"But he was only twenty-one, right? . . . And he died so suddenly. . . ."

"Guess you never know what'll happen. . . ."

"What can you really say? . . . I just can't believe it, that Kōichi's . . ."

"How awful . . ."

"Keep it together. . . ."

"Wasn't that long ago your wife told me he'd gone off to Tokyo and passed the national radiology exam. I was so proud. I said he had a bright future ahead of him. . . . It's such a shame. . . ."

"Poor kiddo . . ."

Osamu, the Maedas' boy from three doors down, had a young woman by his side.

"It happened so suddenly. . . ." he said, eyes downcast.

"Is this your wife?" I asked.

"Yes, this is Akiko. We got married earlier this year. I asked Kōichi to give a speech at the reception, and he . . . he was great. Even at the afterparty, he was so full of energy, getting everyone to sing the school song. I just can't believe that was the last time I'll . . ."

Akiko sighed deeply, pulling a white handkerchief out of her bag and wiping her eyes, then the mix of tears and snot from her nose, before sitting back on her heels again. The babyish roundness of her smooth cheeks only highlighted her grief.

"Kōichi and I were in the same class all the way from elementary to high school, and at roll call his name came right after mine: Maeda, then Mori, always one after the other. In high school, we were in the kendo club together. I was president, he was vice president. . . . He was my closest friend. . . ."

I knew none of this.

My children held little affection for me, the father they rarely saw. And I never knew how to talk to them either.

We shared the same blood, but I meant no more to them than a stranger.

All of a sudden, I wondered who he'd made friends with during his three years in Tokyo, if he'd had a girlfriend— but I could not ask my wife, who was even more inconsolable than I was. And anyway, it was too late to invite his friends or girlfriend to the funeral tomorrow.

The young couple, sticking close to each other, went up to the altar, pressed their hands together in prayer, and began to chant the nembutsu.

Setsuko went over and begged Osamu to take one last look at Kōichi.

Hands together, Osamu bowed on the floor next to the coffin as Setsuko lifted up the white cloth covering Kōichi's face.

He kept his hands pressed together as he came face-to-face with Kōichi.

"He looks just like he's sleeping. . . . I can't believe he's gone," Osamu said, praying again before going back to his wife's side.

As I poured more sake into Osamu's glass, I realized that I'd never had a drink with Kōichi, and now I couldn't even dream of it. Then something swept into the corner of my eye—it was the bird, the one I'd seen on my way to my neighbor's house in the morning, the white-breasted bird, it really was Kōichi after all—but those thoughts might have come to me only after people poured me a few glasses of sake and I was quite drunk.

"Did Kōichi go to the Pure Land?" I heard Setsuko ask the priest, as if she were moaning in pain.

I hadn't noticed that she had sat down next to the priest.

"In the teachings of the True Essence of the Pure Land, we use the phrase 'to pass over' instead of 'to die,' because one is reborn as a Buddha and there is nothing to be saddened by," he began. "Amida Buddha is the Buddha who has sworn to bring all to salvation. Amida Buddha has said that he will bring us to salvation if we simply repeat the nembutsu. Salvation means being reborn in the Pure Land as a Buddha who has attained enlightenment, and being reborn as a Buddha means being reborn on the side of those who offered us salvation. And the dead come back as bodhisattvas, a rank lower than Amida Buddha, to bring salvation to all of us who suffer in this earthly realm, in Amida Buddha's place. This is why we should not think of death as an ending. Those who have passed on are with us, guiding us, when we say the nembutsu. Neither this wake, nor tomorrow's funeral, nor the service forty-nine days after his death are meant to pray for the repose of the deceased, to console or mourn them. No, we are here to express our gratitude for the connection that the deceased gives us to the Buddha. It's the same with the ceremony in a year's time. In a year we will thank the deceased for connecting us to the Buddha, and we will ask him to continue keeping watch over us until the day we can return to the Pure Land and find him."

I could see the tension in Setsuko's hands, resting on her lap. Her fingers seemed to be trying to catch something—

"But Kōichi was barely in his twenties. . . . He died all alone in his apartment in Tokyo, with nobody there with him. . . . The death certificate says he died of illness or natural causes, but the thing is, I don't know how he died or when he died. . . . It's so painful. . . . Did he call out for me?"

The thirty mourners in the room fell silent, and the

grandfather clock struck seven, as if in agreement with the silence.

It was like seeing the invisible hands of time stand still.

The chief priest's voice broke the silence gently.

"Humanity's worst impulse is to imagine those final moments. Those of us left behind wonder whether it was a good death or a bad death. The judgment as to what kinds of deaths are good or bad is entirely our own. In Aizu, there is a statue of Kannon, the bodhisattva of mercy, dedicated to sudden deaths. It originates from when a son went to the temple asking for his parents to pass on without suffering. These days it is no longer sons and daughters who go there but parents. Old men and women pray that they die suddenly so they don't become a burden to their families. When they pass on a few years later from a cardiac arrest, their sons or daughters will always say that their parents had the best of it, that they went on to the Pure Land without becoming a burden to anyone, that there is no more perfect way to die, that they would like to go that way, too. And of course they say that this is a good death.

"But once the services on the seventh day, the forty-ninth day, the hundredth day, and the one-year anniversary have passed, they start saying, 'I wish I'd had one more week with them, just three or four days more, even, to hold their hand, to talk with them.' They come to think that perhaps a sudden death may not be such a good death after all. Nothing has changed about the death—only their judgment. So I cannot tell you what a good death looks like. Amida Buddha committed himself while Kōichi was alive to lead him back to the Pure Land, no matter how he died, and to return Kōichi to us as a bodhisattva," he concluded.

Setsuko began to tremble.

"And now that he's a bodhisattva . . . can I talk to him? Just one more time?"

"If you repeat Namu Amida Butsu . . ."

Setsuko took a deep breath and tried with her right hand to calm the trembling of her left, but she collapsed on the tatami, weeping.

Yoko, sitting seiza in front of the pillar, sobbed even harder.

I wasn't crying. My face was frozen, as though I'd been slapped, and my mouth was so stiff it hurt.

Morning came.

It was the fifth morning since Kōichi had died.

Before, I used to wake up, think about where I was, what I was doing, what day it was, then open my eyes, but afterward I was woken up by one fact alone: Kōichi was dead.

The fact that my only son was dead kept me from sleeping every night, and when I did nod off, exhausted, it broke through my sleep every morning like a kid smashing a baseball through my window.

It was still dark in the house. I heard the chirp of a swallow, followed by the cry of a hawk. Trying to pick up the broken thread of sleep, I was wondering what sort of call the white-breasted bird made when I suddenly noticed a bad smell lingering in the air.

It was, I realized, the smell of food and sake from last night's wake mixed with the smell of decomposition.

It was warm out. The decomposition could've already started—

I was overwhelmed by an emotion, one that I was so tired I could not place. I was exhausted, yet I was still tensed. My whole body was on guard against my emotions. I could not bear it, no more, I could not bear to be sad, to suffer, to be angry—

My stomach ached, clenched like a fist. Still wrapped in

my duvet, I pressed my right hand to my stomach, rubbing it.

The stench was still there.

I closed my eyes and concentrated on breathing.

The smell passed from my nostrils to my lungs, circulating through my body with my blood—I wondered if I would start to decompose now, even as I lived on.

It was over.

It was all over, but I was alive. . . .

I had to live to mourn my son.

To live . . .

After breakfast Setsuko handed me a package wrapped in cloth. I opened it to find mourning clothes. The head of the neighborhood association had lent them to me.

I put on the black kimono and hakama, and Setsuko helped me with the obi.

They brought in the coffin.

We put a thin mat and a pillow inside.

Then we lifted Kōichi up and unfurled the folded sheet he'd been lying on top of.

Setsuko put a shikisho around his neck, and we gently placed him in the coffin.

My mother looked at the coffin, slipped prayer beads into Kōichi's hands, and then pressed her hands together at her chest.

The priest placed a white sheet of paper, folded three times, on Kōichi's body. On it was written: "Namu Amida Butsu."

"As Kōichi did not receive his religious name during his lifetime, I will now, as head priest of the temple with which he was affiliated, pronounce in his stead that he takes the Three Refuges, by which he takes and respects the Three Laws."

We all put our hands together in prayer.

"It is difficult to take human form, but now we have taken it; it is difficult to hear the dharma, but now we have heard it; if we are not liberated in this life, then we will be in the next one; we must all take refuge in the Three Treasures."

The head priest put the razor to Kōichi's hair three times as he continued:

"I take refuge in the Buddha.

"May I, with all beings, understand the great way and make the greatest vow.

"I take refuge in the dharma.

"May I, with all beings, delve deeply into the Sutra Pitaka and gain an ocean of knowledge.

"I take refuge in the sangha.

"May I, with all beings, come into harmony with all beings, entirely without obstruction.

"The ultimate, profound, and mysterious dharma is rarely encountered, even over hundreds, thousands, and millions of centuries, and now we must hear it and see it, accept it and preserve it. May we discover the meaning of the truth of the Tathāgata."

I received a sheet of paper on which was written Kōichi's religious name.

Passed on March 31, 1981
Dharma name: Shaku Junkō
Name in life: Mori Kōichi, age 21

"The Buddha teaches us that we, his followers, must rid ourselves of our worldly name to take his own, Shakyamuni. The character 'shaku' signifies that one has become a follower of the Buddha. The character 'jun,' meaning 'obedient,' signifies obedience to the Buddha's teachings. The final character, 'kō,' is borrowed from his name in life, Kōichi."

The service ended, and it was time for the coffin to leave the house.

We surrounded it and covered Kōichi's body with white chrysanthemums.

The lid was placed on the coffin, and six of our relatives lifted it and carried it to the entrance.

I carried the funeral tablet, inscribed with his post-humous name.

I put on straw sandals with black thongs and went out.

Outside, the light was dazzling.

I knew that the people of Migita were wearing mourning clothes, but the light was so bright that everyone's face was a blank, and I could not tell who was there or what their expressions were.

It must have been a little windy, as cherry petals fell to the ground.

The air smelled of daffodils.

I looked down and saw a large bunch in bloom.

It's spring, I realized.

The only thing I could see clearly was the white wooden hearse, adorned with a copper gabled roof.

I entrusted the funeral tablet to my father and took a step forward to say a word of thanks to those in attendance.

The light was now even more blinding. I opened my mouth to speak, but nothing came out. My legs felt unsteady, as if I were hanging in midair.

My wife and daughter came to my side.

My father spoke in my stead.

"We thank you for coming today to say good-bye to Mori Kōichi. Kōichi's life was short, but it was a happy one, thanks to you. We are full of sorrow, but we hope that the ties that connect us to you will remain unchanged. Thank you again."

When the coffin emerged from the house, all in attendance began to recite the nembutsu.

NAMU AMIDA BUTSU

NAMU AMIDA BUTSU

This invocation of Amida was made with the same sad tone that once made us known as "Kaga whiners" in this region.

NAMU AMIDA BUTSU

NAMU AMIDA BUTSU

My father told me that his great-grandfather, the third generation of the Mori family since their move to Sōma, still spoke the Kaga dialect. He said that in the old days the dead were placed sitting up in coffins that resembled palanquins and were taken to funeral pyres in the mountains, accompanied by all the people of the village reciting the nembutsu. The coffin was placed on the wooden pyre, then lit with wood or straw, the mourners taking turns to keep watch until all that was left were the bones. Then the family members collected the bones by hand—

NAMU AMIDA BUTSU

NAMU AMIDA BUTSU

NAMU AMIDA BUTSU

NAMU AMIDA BUTSU

I carried the funeral tablet and walked at the head of our short procession to the hearse.

Around here, when a son is born, we congratulate the parents by telling them that now they have someone to carry their funeral tablet. "What, this kid?" people say, laughing in response.

I had lost my tablet carrier.

I was the one who carried his tablet.

NAMU AMIDA BUTSU

NAMU AMIDA BUTSU

My hands . . . my feet . . .

My hands carried the tablet, my feet walked toward the hearse.

I had hands and feet, but there was nothing I could do.

NAMU AMIDA BUTSU

NAMU AMIDA BUTSU

Overwhelmed by grief, the grief that had taken everything from me . . .

NAMU AMIDA BUTSU

NAMU AMIDA BUTSU

I had no feeling left in my hands or my feet.

I walked as if sleepwalking.

NAMU AMIDA BUTSU

NAMU AMIDA BUTSU

We borrowed the first character of his name from the title of the crown prince born the same day, February 23, 1960.

And in death, that character remained with him.

Shaku Junkō.

NAMU AMIDA BUTSU

NAMU AMIDA BUTSU

Kōichi would soon be put in the hearse.

The hearse would take him to the crematorium.

Soon Kōichi would be nothing but bones.

NAMU AMIDA BUTSU

NAMU AMIDA BUTSU

NAMU AMIDA BUTSU

NAMU AMIDA BUTSU

The hearse's door closed.

The horn blared to signal that the hearse was about to depart.

———•———

Ding-dong, diiing-dong. "Your attention, please. Smoking while walking in the park is not permitted, as it may pose not only discomfort but also serious health issues to others. Please use the designated smoking areas. We thank you for your cooperation and understanding."

Ding-dong, diiing-dong.

A cloud of smoke hung over the bench where the day-laborer recruiters and the homeless sat.

Construction got you ten thousand yen, demolition

anywhere between ten thousand and twelve thousand, and if electrical work or scaffolding were involved, the rate sometimes went up to between thirteen thousand and fifteen thousand yen a day. If you didn't want dangerous work, and if you had a driver's license and a cell phone, you could register for temp work putting up blinds. Moving work for companies, or setting up or taking down for outdoor events, could net you six thousand to ten thousand yen a day, but anyone who had the drive to do blinds probably wouldn't have been homeless; they would've packed up their tent and moved into a flophouse or gone to the social welfare office and found a way to get benefits.

Truth be told, most of the people living in the park no longer needed to work for the sake of anyone else. Freed from the shackles of doing anything for our wives, children, mothers, fathers, brothers, or sisters, we had to work only enough to be able to eat and drink, which was easier than putting up blinds.

Before, we had families. We had houses. Nobody starts off life in a hovel made of cardboard and tarps, and nobody becomes homeless because they want to be. One thing happens, then another. Some borrow at a high interest rate against their salary and then run off, disappearing in the night; some steal money or hurt others and get banged up in prison, and if they ever get back on the streets, they can't return to their families. There were many homeless men in their forties and fifties who got fired; who were divorced by their wife, who had taken the kids and the house; or who turned to booze or gambling out of desperation and lost all their money, and no matter how many times they went to the employment office, couldn't find the kind of work they wanted.

They were like husks, still wearing suits.

If you fall into a pit, you can climb out, but once you slip from a sheer cliff, you cannot step firmly into a new life again. The only thing that can stop you from falling is the moment of your death. But nonetheless you have to keep living until you die, so there was nothing to do but continue working diligently for your reward.

In the autumn, you could gather the fallen ginkgo nuts from under the trees in the park, wash them, dry them on a rush mat, and sell them.

If you took manga and weekly magazines from the recycling bins at the station and brought them to a secondhand bookshop, you could get a few dozen yen for each. You'd get a better price for magazines with a picture of a young girl in a swimsuit or underwear on the cover than for more serious magazines. There were some who laid their magazines out on a tarp like they were running their own little bookshop, but they sometimes got taken for protection payments by local yakuza, and I'd also heard stories about scuffles between homeless people over magazines, people being pushed onto the train tracks, then getting hit by a train and dying. We were always on edge, dogged by danger and the anxiety that if we had something even for a moment, it could be taken away.

In that regard collecting aluminum cans was much better, because what you collected could be converted into cash the same day. I would take a large plastic bag and walk around picking up discarded cans from the roadside, from the bushes in the park, or from bins. The recycler would pay two yen per can, two hundred yen per hundred, a thousand yen per five hundred, two thousand yen per thousand, and so on.

I don't know how many times I had looked at the statue of Saigō Takamori since I started living in the park at the age of sixty-seven. His body is turned toward Ameyoko Market, gazing out in the direction of the Marui department store. In his right hand is his dog's leash, and with his left he grips the hilt of his sword, though it appears to me that there is far more force in his right hand.

Next to Saigō stood a cockspur coral tree, a South American tree with red petals that is the symbol of Kagoshima Prefecture. Like the bush clover's, its flowers grow at the tips of its branches, but unlike the bush clover's, with its ephemeral white-and-fuchsia petals that blow away in the slightest rain or wind, the coral tree's fallen petals make the ground look like a bloodstained straw mat.

On the other side of the coral tree was the monument to the Shōgitai.

Shige told me all about it.

"This statue of Saigō Takamori, you know, was originally meant to be placed on the plaza of the Imperial Palace, but the idea of putting the statue of a man who had led the Satsuma Rebellion and turned his arrows against the Imperial Army so close to the Imperial Palace seemed indecent to some, so they settled for putting it here, in Ueno Park. And he's not in uniform either, another compromise.

"The monument to the soldiers of the Shōgitai is behind him, and the Shimizu Kannon Temple, less than five minutes away, holds the shells fired by soldiers from the

Nabeshima clan fighting on the imperial side during the Battle of Ueno. This park's a rather strange place.

"The Shōgitai was a group of supporters of the Tokugawa shogunate. There were just seventeen men at the first assembly, but three months later there were over two thousand members, and they established their headquarters here, on this hill in Ueno.

"The people of Edo favored the Shōgitai. Even the girls in the Yoshiwara mocked the Satsuma warriors who were allied with the Imperial Army, calling them 'country bumpkins' and telling them they should join the Shōgitai if they had any courage.

"Edo Castle had been taken without a drop of blood being shed, and the Shōgitai knew that if Tokugawa Yoshinobu had left Edo, then the cause was lost. That's when the Imperial Army, composed mainly of warriors from the Satsuma and Chōshū clans led by Saigō, attacked.

"The confrontation, now seen as the beginning of the Battle of Ueno, took various turns, but the decisive factor is said to be the Nabeshima clan's Armstrong cannons, fired from what is now Tokyo University's Hongō campus. The shells flew over Shinobazu Pond and hit the Shimizu

Kannon Temple, where the Shōgitai were encamped, which is why there are two shells and a print depicting the battle on display there. But in fact none of the shells exploded. Some anecdotes even recount Shōgitai warriors seeing the shells fall and telling everyone to run and take shelter.

"The print on display at the Shimizu Kannon Temple shows the hill of Ueno surrounded by flames from the battle, but this is also slightly misleading. See, the imperial troops brought barrels of oil to set fire to, in order to annihilate the hill of Ueno, which was too closely associated with the Tokugawas—however, the flames happened to reach the buildings of the Kan'ei-ji Temple, which had nothing to do with the conflict.

"The bodies of the Shōgitai fighters who died in the battle lay exposed to the rain on the hill of Ueno for days, even after the flames were extinguished, until a monk from the Entsu Temple in Minami-Senju, who could not bear the piteous sight, and a courageous man named Mikawaya Kozaburo dug a hole there and buried the two hundred and sixty-six corpses. They did so knowing that they were putting their lives at risk.

"Later that year, the Battle of Aizu was fought, in which the Byakkotai, a group of young samurai, famously killed themselves. They were fighting on the side of the Northern Alliance, opposing the restoration of the emperor, but the imperial forces vastly outnumbered them. Aizu Castle fell after a month's siege.

"In less than a decade's time, the rebellion that Saigō launched against the government in his home of Kagoshima had failed, and he committed suicide in a mountain cave in Shiroyama.

"What a coincidence, or rather a twist of fate, it is that this statue of him is located here, in Ueno Park, so close to the memorial to the Shōgitai.

"Kazu, you're from Fukushima, right? You know that originally, back in the Edo period, all of Ueno Park was the grounds of the Kan'ei-ji Temple, right?" he continued. "It was founded by Tenkai, you know, who was from Aizu-Takada in Fukushima. On the other side of the Shimizu Kannon Temple, there's a column containing some of his hair. Tenkai planted Yoshino cherry trees here in Ueno, but that species dates only to the end of the shogunate. So the head of Kan'ei-ji, wanting to re-create the landscape of the past, asked temples from all over to send branches from their best cherry trees for grafting. The ones along the main paths are Yoshino cherries, but the ones at the entrance to the Tokyo Metropolitan Art Museum are weeping cherries from Miharu, in Fukushima. And I'm sure you know about the statue next to the National Museum of Nature and Science, the one of the famous bacteriologist Noguchi Hideyo? He was from Fukushima, too, wasn't he?"

Here, by the statue of Saigō Takamori, is where one most clearly hears sounds from outside the park. When I pushed my bike loaded down with plastic bags full of cans or discarded magazines, I often stopped here and closed my eyes.

The sound of the cars . . . their engines . . . brakes . . . the sound of tires crunching the asphalt . . . the whirring of helicopters . . .

With my eyes shut, the noise of the city lost its place of origin and redirected itself, until I no longer knew if the sounds were coming in at me or if I were moving toward the sounds. I felt as if I were at one with them, sucked up into the air, disappearing without a trace.

The sounds . . .

I felt the rush of air from an oncoming train cut past my ear, then the sound of people getting off and people getting on, even if I couldn't see them . . . a barrage of metal hammerings in my head . . . my eardrums felt like they were going to burst, I curled my body in on itself . . . the panic took my breath away, dried my mouth out. . . .

I stuck my hand in the pocket of my jacket and pulled out a few coins. My hands trembling, I bought a fizzy drink from the vending machine on the platform. With one gulp my panic subsided and I saw the daily activity of the train station around me.

People were waiting along the platform edge for the next train to arrive. I took one more drink, threw the can away, and approached the yellow line.

PLATFORM TWO: THE TRAIN NOW APPROACHING IS FOR IKEBUKURO AND SHINJUKU. FOR YOUR SAFETY PLEASE STAND BEHIND THE YELLOW LINE.

I took one step, then another. My hat was pulled down, so I don't think anyone could see that my eyes were closed. I stood on the yellow line, feeling the ridged paving blocks for the blind through the soles of my shoes, and in the darkness I felt the fear grow and expand. I distinctly heard all the noises around me: people walking in heels, sandals, and boots; people talking on phones as they walked down the platform; impatient murmurs of people waiting for the train; and the clatter from the tracks. . . .

"So I looked on the back of the packaging, right, and saw that the best-before date was that same day. I was like, oh, no, but nobody else seemed to notice, so I didn't say anything either."

"Right, yeah."

"Then the next day, I got to work and got this email. . . ."

"About how the food had gone off?"

"Exactly . . ."

Two men in mourning suits stood chatting between the statue of Saigō and the grave of the Shōgitai. They looked like salarymen. The older one, with salt-and-pepper hair and a surgical mask over his mouth, squinted in the sun while the younger held his briefcase behind him, appearing slightly tense.

"But it's better to be honest, right? I mean, it's better if someone just tells you, like they should, instead of staying silent."

"He said he hadn't put the bento in the fridge, and the next day when he went to eat the food he'd left out overnight, the smell was kind of awful. I had to laugh."

"I mean, it's a best-before date, not an expiration date,

right? If it'd been kept cool, there'd have been no problem. I mean, it'd be just as gross if he'd put it in the microwave, forgotten to take it out, and found it the next day."

The Shōgitai was in rebellion against the shogunate, and as such its name does not appear on the memorial itself, but the metal gates of the fencing around the memorial do bear the character "gi," in rounded relief.

The information board says that the members of the Shōgitai who survived the Battle of Ueno erected this monument at the site where their comrades were cremated, and that their descendants tended the monument for over two centuries; at present the city of Tokyo holds responsibility for its care, as the memorial is designated a historical monument. The artificial flowers left here have lost their color, and their stems are bent and twisted. Someone has left the lid for a tin of mosquito-repelling incense in the incense holder, and a two-liter plastic bottle, cut in half, lies fallen over on its side.

"And lately she's obsessed with baby yams. I'll make a salad or something, and she whines, 'Where are the baby yams? Why aren't there baby yams in this?'"

"She does like the old-fashioned stuff, doesn't she? I mean, I have to admit, boiled baby yams are a nice snack with some sake, and they're really pretty good mixed in with rice."

"The other day she took me to this eel place."

"Oh, no, no, eels are out, they're going extinct, you know. You can't eat them very often. They're endangered, and the catch of the young ones is getting smaller every year, so if we don't let some of the grown eels live, the whole species will die out. I'm not joking."

"We both got rice with one grilled eel fillet on top. And without even asking, she sticks her chopsticks in my bowl and takes half my eel. She said one fillet just wasn't enough for her. Meanwhile I'm left with all this rice and nothing to eat it with, so what else can I do? So there I am, eating rice seasoned with Sichuan pepper. In an eel place."

"How much is rice with grilled eel these days—about two thousand yen?"

"At the place she picked, it was three thousand."

"You must be joking."

"So I told her I'm not going anywhere like that again— oh, no, we're going to the cheapest places, where three thousand yen goes a lot further. So I guess we're going to Gusto, then."

"Gusto?"

"When we go places like that, she always asks for a large serving of rice and then asks for seconds."

"Huh. How old is she?"

"Thirty-two."

"Hardly a growing girl, then."

The two men in funeral wear started off slowly, walking across the expanse toward the Shimizu Kannon Temple.

Standing almost right in the middle of the space, a young woman bent over to tuck the hems of her slim-cut jeans into her brown boots. Her shoulder-length hair swung over her face, obscuring it; her shadow, stretching out from the soles of her boots, looked like a crane in flight.

"When I go to her place, chances are she'll make burgers."

"Really?"

"Anyway, she's always snacking on something—chocolates or sweets."

"They say you really shouldn't overdo it with chocolate."

"Everything in moderation. I mean, I eat sweets, you know. Six sticks of strawberry Pocky is my limit, though. But I don't worry too much about chocolate bars, like the Meiji-brand ones—I mean, they say a little bit is actually good for you, as long as you don't overdo it."

"It's gotta have almonds, otherwise I'm just not interested."

The wind began to blow, and a girl, about four or five years old, emerged from the lacework of light and dark on her pink bike with training wheels. She rode with assurance, tracing circles in the sun. The basket of her bike and her helmet were also pink.

"I think you should eat something sweet every day. A lump of sugar will do, and it's probably the cheapest option."

"Marshmallows."

"What?"

"She's crazy about marshmallows."

"I can't eat marshmallows, they stick to my teeth. Honestly, these days I'm turning into an old man. Just give me some dried sardines, you know, the kind some bartenders put out. I eat them like crazy, like they're candy."

"Oh, yeah, those are great. I don't see how that makes you an old man. You have to have a good set of teeth to get through those."

An old homeless man passed by the Shimizu Kannon Temple. He had a towel tied around his head like a kerchief, and a winter overcoat was attached to his backpack with safety pins.

"When they don't have them in my local supermarket, I keep looking until I find somewhere that does."

"You don't see them around much anymore, do you?"

"Yeah, but if you keep looking, you'll find them eventually. Seek and ye shall find."

A chain saw buzzed. A worker, standing in the basket of a crane on the back of a blue truck, was inside the tunnel formed by the intertwining branches of a zelkova and a ginkgo, cutting according to the instructions of his colleague on the ground below. Another worker gathered the fallen branches and raked up the debris.

"Dried sardines don't have a lot of calories, right? It's a pretty healthy snack, I imagine."

"They're very high in salt, though. I have high blood pressure, so my doctor told me I shouldn't have more than six grams of salt a day, but I like salty food. And dried sardines are the best, especially with sake."

"Smelt, too."

"Oh, yeah, smelt's good, too. . . ."

The two men in black picked up their pace slightly once they got to the signs in front of Suribachiyama and headed off toward the park entrance of Ueno Station.

There are two signs in front of Suribachiyama. The

white one has a message from the Ueno Police, in eye-catching red type: ENTRANCE FORBIDDEN AT NIGHT. The stainless-steel sign is from the Taitō District Educators Association, explaining the mound's name.

ERECTED ABOUT FIFTEEN HUNDRED YEARS AGO, THE SURIBACHI MOUND IS THOUGHT TO BE A FUNERAL MOUND. IT CONTAINS POTTERY FROM THE YAYOI ERA, AS WELL AS FRAGMENTS OF HANIWA FUNERAL CYLINDERS. THE NAME SURIBACHI (LITERALLY 'MORTAR') COMES FROM THE SHAPE OF THE MOUND, WHICH RESEMBLES AN OVERTURNED MORTAR.

At the top of Suribachi Mound there is a circular open space, surrounded by tall, bare-branched ginkgoes and zelkovas, which have such dense leaves from spring to autumn that the view beyond is obscured.

If you do look through the branches, however, you can see the green enclosure around the Masaoka Shiki Memorial Baseball Field, named after the poet who played baseball here when he was a student. And on days when kids' or adults' teams are playing, you can hear the players call out to each other, the noise of balls hitting bats and gloves, and the cheers and shouts of spectators and family members; but today there is nothing to listen to.

Listen.

To speak is to stumble, to hesitate, to detour and hit dead ends. To listen is straightforward. You can always just listen.

I hear a listless sort of screeching.

Possibly the first cicadas of the year.

Could be a Kaempfer cicada. . . .

Or maybe it's not a cicada, maybe it's a katydid or something else. . . .

A bird crows, hidden somewhere in the trees; three sparrows perch on the old-fashioned lamp in the middle of the space, chirrup, chirrup, chi-chi, chirrup. . . .

The sound of the chain saw pruning tree limbs around the statue of Saigō Takamori continues.

I can hear a lawn mower over near the baseball field, too.

The wind whips around, rustling through the leaves of the trees, and now I can see the tent city full of homeless people. It's surrounded by a green fence with a tarpaulin over the grating. There's a design printed on the tarp—of a blue sky with seagulls and big columns of clouds floating, a hill with two trees, a two-story house with a red roof and smoke coming out of the chimney and two white-spotted dogs running toward it, but there are no people in the design.

The three sparrows that were perched on the lamppost before have now gone. I am haunted by this day, today, and regardless of what I am now, I would have liked to exchange a glance with someone, anyone, even a sparrow.

A burlap sack sits under the lamppost, next to a pile of dead leaves. It would take only a broom and a shovel to gather them and put them in the bag, but there is no broom, no shovel, and nobody, nobody, nobody. . . .

No, someone is there. A man with a receding hairline, faceup on one of the three sarcophagus-like stone benches surrounding the area. Purple sweatshirt, beige trousers, newspapers spread underneath him, covered with a green sweater. His hands are crossed over his solar plexus, and his feet, clad in black shoes, are so perfectly close that they might as well be tied together. His eyes, lips, and Adam's apple are motionless. I can't hear him breathing in or out, so perhaps he is no longer alive. If he is indeed dead, it hasn't been long—

By his feet is a large, transparent trash bag full of aluminum cans. Those three hundred cans are worth six hundred yen. With six hundred yen, you could go to a public bath, or to a manga café or internet café and have a shower, or get a hot bowl of beef on rice at Yoshinoya, or have a real coffee in a real café.

But you can't sell the cans in this state. They have to be crushed one by one with a hammer. In the winter it hurt because my hands were numbed by the cold, even with gloves on, and in the summer the smell of the juice or sports drinks lingering in the empty cans clung to every part of my body, nauseating me.

The man looked so neatly turned out that people with homes would not have guessed it, but the fact that he was sleeping like the dead on a stone bench with a bag of cans at his feet told me that he was almost certainly homeless.

Shige always looked impeccable.

One time, I'm not sure when, exactly—it was cold so it must've been winter—I was heading back to my shelter with my bike after a day spent collecting cans and magazines when Shige called me over to his hut for a drink, although he normally didn't touch the stuff.

I pushed open the veneered door with a cat flap at the bottom, set my shoes to one side, and went in. It was the first time I'd been inside someone else's hut. I think it was the first time Shige had received a visitor, too, because he apologized for how small his place was and stroked Emile with an unjustified embarrassment. Emile purred loudly, his tail stuck in the air.

I noticed a clock and a mirror hanging on the wall, as well as a calendar with certain days circled in red or blue, and I thought then that Shige must've worked in a local government office or a school in his previous life; he was such a methodical person.

"It's so cold I thought we might drink the sake hot instead," he said, putting a pot on his gas stove and filling it with water from a large plastic bottle before adding the two single-serving containers of sake.

His shelves were full of books he'd picked up from the streets, but with only the dim flashlight hanging from the ceiling I could not read the titles on the spines. And even if I had been able to read them, I don't expect I would've known what they were.

"Sorry, I don't have much in the way of snacks," Shige said, setting out a plate of peanuts and dried cuttlefish. Then he turned to Emile, who was rubbing the edge of the table with his head and purring. "They say that if you feed a cat cuttlefish, it will paralyze it, and that's no superstition. Cuttlefish and shellfish contain an enzyme that destroys vitamin B1, and if a cat eats a lot of either, a B1 deficiency will make it start staggering around. Heat destroys the enzyme, but dried cuttlefish will absorb up to ten times its weight in water in the stomach, which makes it difficult to digest anyway. It can cause vomiting and sudden gastric dilation, too, making their stomachs hurt. I have something much better for you, Emile," he concluded, getting a packet of kibble and a can of tuna down from a bag of supplies hanging from the ceiling. Even before Shige had finished mixing the two in a saucer with a spoon, Emile began eating greedily.

"Watching him eat like that always makes me hungry. Around here it's all about Emile. When I get some money, first I buy food for him, and whatever's left is for my own needs. This place is too small for two people, but it's just the right size for one person and one cat."

While we'd both been watching Emile eat, the pot had come to a boil. Shige tried to take both bottles out quickly, but they were too hot to handle with bare hands.

"They say hot sake's best either at body temperature or

warmed by the heat of the sun, but I'm afraid this is so hot it'll burn our mouths," he said, putting on gloves. He grabbed the two bottles and removed their lids. "Well, let's have a drink anyway."

I stuttered a few words of thanks, holding the glass in my hands with the sleeves of my sweater pulled down for protection. Looking at the photo of bonsai on the reverse side of the label, I took a sip.

"Oh, that's hot!" Shige said.

"This'll warm us up for sure," I said.

I didn't tell him that I didn't drink.

When my glass was about half empty, to where the words A CUP OF HAPPINESS are on the label, Emile jumped up onto Shige's lap. He had finished eating and cleaning himself and now lay down.

Shige stroked him, and his silence suggested that there was something he wanted to say that he couldn't quite find the words for. His face was scarlet, so I assumed he was not much of a drinker either.

"Today is my son's thirty-second birthday. We had him when I was forty after trying for a long time, and he's an only child. . . ."

It felt like a long wait until he next spoke. Being in an

enclosed space, face-to-face with someone who was my age yet had had such a different life, was terrifying to me. I looked over at the part of his shelter that served as something like the kitchen, at the frying pan and the ladle hanging there, and then I looked out the window cut into the cardboard, drinking my sake. It was now cooler than either body temperature or if it had been warmed by the sun.

"He was ten when I left. I guess he has his own family now. I might even be a grandfather. . . ."

He spoke as if he were taking a step back rather than forward.

"I ran away because I had made a mistake. One that meant I couldn't hold my head up in public anymore. People must've talked behind my wife's and my son's backs, and I imagine that they suffered a great deal." He squinted and suddenly looked much older.

I finished my drink while he was talking. Now that I had nothing left to drink, I felt uncomfortable—as if I were naked in front of him, but I had no desire to confide in him, to tell him that I was also born in 1933 or that my son would be forty-five if he were still alive.

I only struggled not to let drunkenness lead me into sadness.

The memories of the past that I could not get rid of were all contained in a box. And time had sealed the lid. A box whose lid is sealed by time should not be opened. Were it opened, I would be plunged at once into the past.

"I'm sure they're both angry with me. And they're not the only ones I've caused trouble for. . . ." He spoke hesitantly, as if he were delirious with fever, and he did not sound like himself to me.

"I can't go home again, even when I'm dead. I've destroyed everything that could be used to identify me, so that my family won't be notified. When I die, I imagine that I'll end up in an unmarked grave," he said, and sighed deeply before straightening up and returning to his normal way of speaking.

"They say a typhoon is going to hit tomorrow. Have you made plans for where to go, Kazu?"

"No, I intend to stay in my hut," I said, straightening my back, too, and accidentally sounding too formal.

He asked me then if I would join him at the library instead. He explained that the Taitō Ward Main Library was on Kototoi-dōri toward the Sumida River and how to get there via Showa-dōri. I could read newspapers and magazines, watch videos or listen to records in the audiovisual section, or read books about history and culture. "Even if you stayed there all day, from nine A.M. to eight P.M., nobody would say a word to you about it," he assured me, but something about the intensity with which he grasped the empty glass of sake between his long fingers frightened me. I said that I was not good at reading and left Shige's hut.

I think he was looking for someone. Someone who would listen. If I had asked, I'm sure he would've told me anything. If I had shown him that I was ready to listen—or if we'd had one or two more cups of warm sake—he would have told me what mistake he'd made, and something like friendship could have developed between us; but those who hear another's secret are obliged to share one of their own. Secrets are not necessarily hidden things. Events that do not bear hiding become secrets when one chooses not to speak of them.

I spent my life thinking about people who were not there. People who were not with me, people who were no longer in this world. I never felt entitled to speak of the absent to those who were there, even to my own family. I could not alleviate the weight of my memories of those who were absent by speaking of them. I did not want to betray my own secrets.

A month after the night I drank sake with Shige, I was gone.

Was Shige sad about it?

The old woman with hair like a white bird's nest stood in front of the tent village, smoking a Hi-Lite and talking. She said that Shige had been found cold in his hut—

When did he die? Where was he buried? Someone must've sold the books in his hut to a secondhand shop, but where was Emile? Had another homeless person taken him in? Or had he been captured and euthanized by animal control?

I thought that once I was dead, I would be reunited with the dead. That I would see, close up, those who were far away, touch them, and feel them at all times. I thought something would be resolved by death. I believed that at the final moment the meaning of life and death would appear to me clearly, like a fog lifting—

But then I realized that I was back in the park. I was not going anywhere, I had not understood anything, I was still stunned by the same numberless doubts, only I was now outside life looking in, as someone who has lost the capacity to exist, now ceaselessly thinking, ceaselessly feeling—

The man lying on top of the stone bench still hadn't opened his eyes. A cat appeared from out of nowhere and scratched its claws on the tree near the man's head, but the noise did not seem to reach him.

That day—time has passed. Time has ended. But that time is scattered here and there like spilled pushpins. As I am unable to take my eyes away from that glance at sadness, all I can do is suffer—

Time does not pass.

Time never ends.

A lukewarm, damp breeze licked over me, the limbs of the trees gently bowing, shaking drops of rain to the ground. Though there was still some time until dusk, the flow of people had suddenly stopped. Even the sound of chain saws and lawn mowers now sounded like a part of the silence. Day by day the sunlight was getting stronger and the shadows of the trees shorter; before long it would be monsoon season and the cicadas would start to call.

From around the corner appeared a woman, perhaps a student, wearing blue jeans and a white, short-sleeved blouse, who slowed in front of a poster for the Ueno Royal Art Museum, gave it a glance, and then, with a glum look, walked off toward the station.

The poster showed a large drawing of a pink rose. The bloom, which fanned out layer after layer like a cabbage's leaves, grew redder toward the middle, leading one to imagine that the center, hidden by those petals, was as red as a scraped knee. And on the yellowish, supple stems and the calyxes of the buds that had not yet opened, the artist had drawn the points of little thorns.

In the gift shop in the lobby of the Ueno Royal Art Museum, ladies in their sixties and seventies walked around the rose-patterned handkerchiefs, coin purses, postcards, sticky notes, and fans, perusing, picking things up, and purchasing them.

The exhibition displayed pictures of roses by Redouté, a painter in the French court active at the start of the nineteenth century; it showed 169 of his works in total.

Two women, looking at the paintings without paying much attention, walked slowly as they spoke about something completely unrelated to roses, guided by the signs in the museum.

"Life has taken a strange turn for me these last few

weeks. Takeo won't let anyone else get involved. Takeo manages everything, you know. I haven't been looking after him, so I have no say, and it costs money to put someone in the hospital, he says."

"Well, I think he's right about some things, certainly. But being right isn't all there is to life."

"I thought about asking him but I know he wouldn't listen. . . ."

"I mean, you say it's your husband's family, but at the end of the day that's still not your own family."

"That's what he said, that it wasn't a stranger's business. So I said, 'Am I a stranger, then?'"

"You are. I mean, you've got no blood ties."

ROSA GALLICA PURPURO-VIOLACEA MAGNA, THE BISHOP ROSE: DEEPLY COLORED, TINGED WITH BLACK, THE OUTER PETALS OF THIS ROSE TURN UP ONCE PAST ITS PEAK, WHILE THE INNER PETALS, JUST BEGINNING TO BLOOM, ARE PURPLISH RED. . . .

"Are you going to go to Nagano again?"

"Back to Yatsugatake? No, never again. I can't. Takeo and I always went together anyway."

ROSA PUMILA, THE ROSE OF LOVE: AT THE CENTER OF THIS
FIVE-PETALED PURPLISH PINK FLOWER IS ITS YELLOW
STAMEN, SHINING LIKE A TORCHLIGHT. . . .

"He calls me up just to insist that he doesn't have de-
mentia."

"Well, if he did, he wouldn't call, then, would he?"

"But, honestly, he's like a shadow of himself. He orders
me around like a subordinate. 'Mieko, put the kettle on!'"

"Life's a rich tapestry."

"It's awful, and for everyone around him, too, it's just—"

ROSA GALLICA VERSICOLOR, "ROSA MUNDI," THE DAPPLED
ROSE OF PROVENCE: RED-AND-WHITE-STRIPED PETALS LIKE
A TULIP, THE YELLOW POLLEN OF THE STAMEN COATS THE
STILL-UNOPENED PETALS IN THE MIDDLE, LENDING
THEM A PALE YELLOW TINGE. . . .

ROSA GALLICA REGALIS, ROSIER GRANDEUR ROYALE:
SPREADING UNEVENLY, UNDULATINGLY, THE PALE PINK
PETALS ARE NUMEROUS, FORMING A LUXURIOUS TUFT
THAT HIDES THE CENTER OF THE FLOWER. . . .

"Takeo sent us a set of boil-in-bag pouches of curry and stew. Now, what do you think that was for?"

"It's a bit early for Bon presents."

"The wrapping said 'In gratitude.'"

"In gratitude? For what? Maybe he's trying to say that he wants to settle this thing once and for all. I mean, you two have been separated for nearly six months now, no?"

"It was S&B curry, the ones that are kind of restaurant style."

"What's the line from that ad? 'Holiday food's fine, but don't forget the curry'?"

"That was House curry. Anyway, I thought why not keep them? You never know when the next big earthquake might hit."

"It goes really well with an onigiri."

"Curry and an onigiri?"

"Oh, it's delicious!"

ROSA ALBA REGALIS, GREAT MAIDEN'S BLUSH: COLORED WHITE WITH THE MEREST HINT OF PINK, ITS PETALS TURN IN TOWARD THE CENTER, INCREASING IN DEPTH AS IF THEY ARE BEING SUCKED IN. . . .

ROSA ALBA FLORE PLENO, THE ROSE OF THE HOUSE
OF YORK: THE PURE WHITE ROSE'S PETALS EMIT A
PEARLESCENT LUSTER. IN THE WARS OF THE ROSES,
THE HOUSE OF YORK CARRIED THIS ROSE

the explanatory panel reads, but the two ladies just flapping their jaws pass by the paintings of roses, their eyes glazed and downcast.

"You know, you really should have a proper talk with Takeo sooner rather than later."

"But I've got our son and his wife in the house, and the grandkids, too."

"Well, then keep him away when the kids are there. Have him over in secret when nobody's there, or have him meet you at a café or somewhere else."

"It's really not the kind of conversation you can have in a café."

"How about the park, then? You talk as you walk around Ueno Park, and then you don't have to worry about anyone else watching you."

"We're not teenagers. It would look ridiculous."

"Then what are you going to do?"

"No, you know, I have to do it at home. It's the only way. . . ."

ROSA GALLICA FLORE MARMOREO, THE MARMOREAL ROSE
OF PROVENCE: ITS DOUBLE PETALS WITH A COLOR
SOMEWHERE BETWEEN ORANGE AND PINK ARE
SPECKLED WITH WHITE LIKE A FAWN. . . .

ROSA INERMIS, THE THORNLESS WHIRLPOOL ROSE: ITS
COLOR IS AMBIGUOUS AND COULD BE DESCRIBED AS
APRICOT OR RASPBERRY. THE PETALS OPEN CARELESSLY,
MAKING IT LOOK MUCH LIKE THE PAPER FLOWERS STUCK TO
CLASSROOM BLACKBOARDS AT GRADUATION, FIVE OR SIX
SHEETS OF TISSUE PAPER PUT TOGETHER, FOLDED IN PEAKS
AND VALLEYS LIKE AN ACCORDION, BOUND IN THE MIDDLE
WITH A RUBBER BAND, THEN EACH SHEET OPENED UP. . . .

There were no roses in my hometown. The first rose I ever held was a white one, at Shinsekai.

While in Tokyo I worked nonstop with no regard for my personal appearance, never drinking or gambling, never chatting to female salesclerks as much as I should have, thinking that any Tokyo woman would laugh at my accent.

I started going to Shinsekai, a cabaret, when I was around fifty. It had been three years since Kōichi had passed away.

I was working on a site for a new sports ground in Hirosaki. One evening when my shift ended, I walked through the red-light district with its competing bars until the pink neon sign reading SHINSEKAI stopped me in my tracks.

If the version of me that existed a decade before had seen me then, he wouldn't have believed it. I went in alone and was shown to a table. Nobody batted an eye at my muddy work clothes.

As I sat on the sofa waiting for the hostess, I stared at the white rose in the stem vase next to the ashtray on my table. Wondering if it was a fake, I pulled the flower out and lifted it to my nose, when suddenly a hostess sat down next to me. "Sorry to keep you waiting. I'm Junko."

I hurried to return the rose to its vase.

"Do you like roses?" she asked. Her accent sounded like mine, and without thinking I answered back in dialect.

"I thought it was fake. I was just having a good sniff."

Junko laughed, her waist-length hair shaking gently, and then she made me a whiskey with water. She was from Namie in Fukushima. We talked at random about home—about Ukedo Port, the Sōma Nomaoi, the nuclear plant she said her brothers worked at, Hamadōri—and the cabaret, dark already at the best of times, became pitch-black as a giant mirror ball began to turn, small flashes of light reflecting on Junko's pale face and plump chest.

When you do physical labor, you sleep like the dead, so I have no recollection of ever having a truly dreamlike dream, but Junko was like my dream woman.

"Dance cheek to cheek with me?"

"I don't know how to dance."

"Don't worry."

Junko took my hand and led me to the center of the floor.

The maroon carpet absorbed all sound of our steps. It was as though my feet weren't even touching the floor.

The music played, but it was even quieter than the night.

I listened carefully; I could hear the sound of my own heart beating and Junko whispering, "Put your arms around me."

It was the first slow dance I'd had in my life.

Her eyes were moist.

Her hands were on my lower back.

Her hair was brushing against me.

Her earrings were quivering.

Her breasts were soft against my chest.

Her perfume smelled the same as the white rose on the table, a soft scent with a touch of lemon and salt water.

My whole body shook.

I felt I was at sea.

As I shook, I felt as if I were being simultaneously unleashed and enveloped.

When I was in Hirosaki, I always went to Shinsekai.

I always asked for Junko. Sometimes I would wait until the club closed to drop her off by taxi at her apartment building, but I never paid to take her on a date, and I never crossed over the line from being just another regular customer.

At sixty I decided to stop working away from home and returned to Yazawa.

On my last day, I took a bouquet of white roses to Shinsekai.

Standing in front of Junko, I handed her the bouquet and said good-bye. "Thank you," she said, pressing the white roses to her face, engulfing herself in the strong scent. Sadness welled up in my throat, but I didn't cry. I pulled her pale arm from the bouquet and shook her hand, and her arm moved lifelessly.

And with that I never saw Junko again. I never called or wrote. I don't know if Shinsekai is still there or not, nor what Junko is doing, or even if she's still alive. . . .

"If you'd like some plants for your house, then take some, please."

"I just don't have time for plants. They need lots of care, you know? Oh, Tomoko's father died suddenly, did you hear? Seems like it was quite a shock to her—she hasn't gotten out of bed for ages, apparently. . . ."

"That doesn't mean she can't leave the house at all, surely."

"She might not come to the class reunion this year."

"She'll be there, I know she will. She got the award for perfect attendance."

Another two women, also in their early sixties, chatted as they looked at a picture of Centifolia roses—"Centifolia" meaning "hundred-leaved."

The Centifolia rose, famously clasped by Marie Antoinette in a portrait, is called "the painter's rose" and is in the first of Redouté's series of paintings. Once too many petals grow, the stamen and pistil will degenerate and die, so it can propagate only by grafting. . . .

"You have a sideboard, don't you? You could put it there."

"In the Japanese-style room?"

"No, the altar room, of course."

"We don't have one. When my father died, Mom bought a big old altar and told us about it afterward. I was so annoyed."

"I guess it'll shake when there's an earthquake, and it might be a bit scary, but what can you do?"

"I'd have to put it next to the TV."

"If you put a sideboard next to the TV, the height would just about be right, too. The TV stand is adjustable, isn't it?"

"Maybe I have something at home that'll do."

"I really think you should buy a proper sideboard."

"Want to go look at some together?"

"Tomorrow?"

"No rush."

———

ROSA CENTIFOLIA MUTABILIS, UNEQUALED ROSE: ITS ROUND,
BULBOUS GROUPINGS OF BLOOMS ARE AS PALE AS A WHITE
WOMAN'S SKIN, THE OUTER PETALS ALONE AS RED AS IF
THEY HAD BEEN SWEPT WITH BLUSH. . . .

ROSA INDICA CRUENTA, BLOOD-CRIMSON ROSE OF BENGAL:
CHOCOLATE-TINGED RED, THE PETALS ON THE VERGE OF
FALLING, HANGING DOWN LIKE A DOG'S TONGUE . . . THE
NOTICEABLY SERRATED LEAVES ARE TURNED UP, SHOWING
THEIR GRAY UNDERSIDES. . . .

ROSA INDICA, THE BEAUTIFUL LADY OF BENGAL: BREAK
OPEN THE RED BUDS AND THE DEEP PINK PETALS SPILL
OUT. ITS LEAVES HEAVE LIKE THE PECTORAL FIN OF A
STINGRAY, ITS LARGE, DOWNWARD-FACING THORNS
THE COLOR OF A BLOOD BLISTER. . . .

As if they had been waiting for their oldest son, their tablet
carrier, to return home, my father died, followed by my

mother. Both were over ninety, so it was their time, I suppose. Our family grave was on top of a hill from which
Migitahama Beach was visible. Their urns were placed
next to that of Kōichi, lost at the tender age of twenty-one.

I think if one were to count all the days I had spent with
my wife, Setsuko, after thirty-seven years of marriage with
me mainly away from home, they would not even add up
to a year. Setsuko had given birth to and raised our two
children, put her much younger brothers through university, seen Yoko get married, cared for our aging parents
while working in the fields, and had steadily built up sav-
ings for us. We also had seventy thousand yen a month
from our national pensions, which we could live on until
the time came, so after a discussion we decided to have
our rotting roof, walls, and plumbing repaired.

Yoko, who lived in Sendai, had three children, and
during their summer and winter holidays they would come
to stay with us. The oldest was a fourteen-year-old girl, followed by two boys, eleven and nine. Our neighbors said
how perfect it was to have one little princess and two wild
boys.

The youngest, Daisuke, looked just like Kōichi when he

was little, but neither my wife nor I ever said a word about it to each other.

It had been raining since the morning.

I couldn't help remembering the day nineteen years before, when Setsuko and I had gone together, while Kōichi was being autopsied, to the apartment where he'd lived for three years and had lain on the futon, where he died, until the next morning.

It was the day of the forty-ninth-day memorial service for Mrs. Chiyo from two doors down, and it was custom for the women of the neighborhood association to make the food for the reception. Setsuko had been out since early morning to prepare.

In the evening we changed into funeral wear and went to join the other mourners. The priest from Shoen-ji Temple led the service. We faced the altar, hands clasped in prayer, and chanted together the Sukhavativyuha Sutra and the nembutsu hymn.

Katsunobu, the chief mourner, had gone off to Tokyo looking for work with a group of other locals after graduating from middle school, worked at Mitsubishi Electric's factory in Ōfuna, and returned to our hometown after retirement to live with his widowed mother, leaving his wife and children back in Kanagawa.

"It barely seems possible, but it has already been forty-nine days since she passed. My mother loved talking and taking care of others, and I feel her absence most at dinnertime, but she had eighty-eight happy years thanks to all of you present here today, and I know that she has been reborn in the Pure Land now, which gives me some comfort.

"As you know, my family is in Kanagawa, and I will return to them once I've finished settling things here, but I will be back for the rest of the memorial services, so I hope for your continued friendship and support. We have only a small meal to offer you, but please stay as long as your time allows. Thank you all for coming today."

The meal began, and as we ate root vegetables stewed in soy sauce, kinpira gobō, pickles, potato salad, and onigiri with vegetables mixed in, Katsunobu and I drank so much sake together that I was unsteady on my feet. I don't remember how I got home, but I went to sleep without any dinner, in the bed that Setsuko had laid out for me.

The sound of the rain woke me.

Setsuko always got up early, so by the time I usually woke at seven, she was already done with the laundry and cleaning the floors, and the smell of miso soup and steaming rice would waft from the kitchen.

That morning there was no such smell. . . .

I heard the sound of water gushing from the rainspouts.

It must be a rather big downpour. . . .

The light leaking in through the curtains stained the walls of the house with rain.

I turned my head and saw Setsuko asleep next to me on her futon.

I reached out an arm to wake her. She was cold—

Her arm, peeking out from the top of the duvet, was cold.

In shock I got up, pulled the duvet back, and tried to shake her, but rigor mortis had already begun to set in.

Struggling, I slammed my eyes shut, knitting my brows.

"Why?" The word slipped out of my mouth.

My heart was pounding violently, and the inside of my head was like an illuminated red void. I looked around the house, hoping this was a dream, but everything was where it should be. This was reality. The sound of the grandfather clock that I knew so well reverberated through the house, but I was in such shock I could not count the number of chimes. I looked at the dial. The short hand was near the seven, the long hand was near twelve.

"It's seven," I moaned at Setsuko.

There was the wake, funeral, farewell ceremony, coffin, cremation, bone picking, the return of her remains, notification of death, gifts for the temple and neighborhood association, procedures to return her health-insurance card and stop her pension, liquidation of her estate, the memorial service on the forty-ninth day after her death, laying her ashes to rest—as I did these things which I still could not come to terms with at all, one by one, everything connected with Setsuko's death came to an end.

Opening the storage vault under the tombstone at the family grave, I shifted my father's and mother's remains to one side and placed Setsuko's remains next to Kōichi's, and at that moment the keening of a cicada somewhere in the pine trees above me rang out.

It was the first cry of a Kaempfer cicada, the first to emerge every year at the start of the rainy season.

I remembered how, a few days before she died, Setsuko had said while folding the washing, "I just have the feeling I'm gonna die when the cicadas are singing," and I sank to my hands and knees crying. Did she cry out, "It hurts, help"?—would she have lived if I'd called an ambulance right away?—but I had been drunk and sound asleep, and I didn't realize that my wife, right next to me, was taking her last breath. It was the same as if I'd killed her, I thought.

After the sutras from the priest, once we had all offered incense in order of relation starting with me and the interment ceremony was over, Setsuko's brother, Sadao, offered me some words of comfort. "No matter how we grieve, the dead will not return. You two had those last seven years together, just the two of you, like a honeymoon. You should think of how happy Setsuko was." But I kept chewing over what my mother had said when Kōichi died: "You never did have any luck, did you?"

She did complain sometimes about her back or her knees hurting, but Setsuko took pride in being a hard worker and having a strong body, and now that she was dead at the age of sixty-five—why did it always have to go this way?—an anchor of indignation sank to the bottom of my heart, and I could no longer cry.

My daughter, Yoko, was worried about me, so she sent my granddaughter, Mari, who had just started work as a nurse at an animal hospital in Haramachi, over to visit occasionally, and in the end Mari, saying she was worried about me, too, moved out of her apartment and in with me.

She brought along Kotaro, a small brown dog with a long body and who barked a lot. Mari said he had been left chained to the fence around the animal hospital. She'd made a flyer looking for someone to foster him and pinned it on the noticeboard at work, but nobody came forward to take him in, so Mari had taken him home herself.

Mari was a good girl. Every morning she made me toast and fried eggs or ham and eggs. She was especially sweet when she turned her head to look down at the dog, sitting patiently at her feet, to talk to him or give him a smile. At seven in the morning, she'd put the dog in the passenger seat of her car and drive down Highway 6 to Haramachi. She often didn't get back from work until late, so I made my own lunch and dinner. Cooking and cleaning were no trouble for me after years of dormitory living when I'd been working away from home, but soon after Bon was over, I found myself unable to sleep. Kōichi and Setsuko had both been taken in their sleep—at night, when I lay down in my bed, I felt a chill over my body, my saliva felt sticky, my tongue sour. All the nerves running through my body were tensed, and I didn't feel ready to sleep. Realizing that my hands were becoming numb, I closed my eyes and tried to calm my breathing, but having my eyes closed scared me. I was not afraid of ghosts. Nor was I afraid of death or dying. I was afraid of living this life not knowing when it might end. It did not seem possible to resist this weight pressing down on my entire body, nor to bear it.

It was a rainy morning.

"Oh, it's muggy," Mari said, half opening the screened window. A damp wind and the sound of rain came rolling in. The smell of rain in my nose, I ate the scrambled eggs and toast that Mari had made, then said good-bye to her and the dog from the entrance hall as they drove off. She's just turned twenty-one, I thought. She shouldn't be tied down here with her granddad.

"Sorry for leaving so suddenly. Grandpa's gone to Tokyo.

I won't be coming back to the house again. Please don't come looking for me. Thank you for always making me such nice breakfasts," I wrote on a piece of paper to leave for her; then I took the black carry-all I'd used for work out of a closet and put my personal belongings in it.

At Kashima Station I got on the Jōban Line, and I got off at Ueno, the last stop. When I surfaced from the park exit ticket gates, it was raining in Ueno, too. The crossing light was green, so I didn't bother with my umbrella and crossed the road. I looked up at the night sky. I saw the rain falling from the sky in large drops, and my rain-drenched eyelids quivered. I decided to wait the night out under the awning of the Tokyo Metropolitan Festival Hall, but as I listened to the sound of rain hitting regularly against the ground, exhaustion came over me and I fell asleep with my bag for a pillow.

That was the first night I spent sleeping rough.

———·———

ROSA MULTIFLORA CARNEA, FLESH-COLORED ROSE THAT BLOOMS IN TUFTS: ITS PINK FLOWERS, SMALL AND ROUND LIKE THE BELLS THAT CHILDREN CHIME AT SCHOOL

CONCERTS, BLOOM AS IF GATHERED TOGETHER, THE
FLOWER'S RECEPTACLES HANGING HEAVILY. . . .

———•———

ROSA PIMPINELLIFOLIA FLORE VARIEGATO, HUNDRED
ÉCU D'ARGENT BURNET: ITS SLIM RECEPTACLE, CLOSELY
CROWDED WITH BLACK THORNS LIKE A HAIRY
CATERPILLAR, STRETCHES OUT PROUDLY, CROWNED
WITH REGAL STAMENS. HALF OF ITS SINGLE-LAYERED
WHITE PETALS ARE COPPER RED, AS IF THEY HAD
BEEN SOAKED IN BLOOD. . . .

———•———

ROSA DUMETORUM, THE THICKET ROSE: THIS FIVE-PETALED
ROSE, WITH ITS PALE APRICOT, HEART-SHAPED PETALS, IS
LIKE A BUTTERFLY JUST TAKEN TO THE WING. . . .

The backgrounds have been left blank, nothing drawn. One
cannot tell when or where each rose is blooming, whether
it is in a garden or a flowerpot; whether it is sunny, or

cloudy, or raining; whether it is morning, or noon, or night; whether it is spring, or summer, or autumn. Redouté, the man who painted these roses, died over a hundred seventy years ago. And the rose bushes that he studied are more than likely no longer living either. But once, somewhere, those roses were in bloom. And once, somewhere, a painter lived. And now, through these pieces of paper divorced from the reality of the past, like fantastical flowers that do not exist in our world, these roses bloom.

"You know that beef-stew place over there? I went a while back, and they weren't open."

"They close on Tuesdays, you know."

"We should go sometime for their 'lightweight' breakfast special."

"How about now?"

"Can't today, I'm afraid. He hates it when I eat out for dinner."

"Oh, mine doesn't mind eating alone. I just have to give him a call."

"That doesn't swing at my house. Even when I was working, I had to make him lunch every day."

"What a bother. Well, then I guess you'd better be off to get the shopping."

"I've already got everything I need at home, but you're right, I'd better be going."

"Right then, let's go."

The two women, around the same age as Setsuko was when she died, walked toward the exit.

———— · ————

The sky looked menacing again. Or was it just that the sun was obscured? The sunlight that remained was weakening, and when the two women turned a corner and disappeared, the landscape suddenly spread aimlessly, without beginning or end.

Today was still today, not yet opening toward tomorrow. Hidden within today was a past longer than the present. . . . I felt as if I were listening to signs of that past, and equally I felt as if I were closing my ears off to it. . . .

Suddenly I heard someone sigh.

It was a sigh I'd heard before.

It was a man in his fifties, sobbing as he told his life story, something out of the ordinary for the homeless.

"After university I went to work at a real estate company. I got contract after contract for resort condos worth nearly a hundred million yen, and I was on salary plus commission, so sometimes I was taking home eight hundred thousand yen a month. But that took a turn. The bubble burst, and within three years the company folded. My severance pay was set at only twenty percent of my annual income, and I couldn't pay my loans back. If I'd known this kinda thing could happen, I'd have taken what I could get in the first round of redundancies and found a new job quick. But I was loyal to my company. I kept saying it's just a recession, it can't last that long, and that naïveté is what did me in. I hit the bottom. Splat. With my wife's support, maybe I could've gotten back on my feet again, but then, like a bolt from the blue, she hit me with divorce papers. Like biting the hand that feeds you. I didn't know what to say. All I could do was silently give my seal of consent, but I guess our relationship was falling apart long before the bubble burst. On weeknights I'd be out in Ginza and Roppongi, and Saturdays and Sundays I was golfing with clients, so this was my punishment for neglecting her. My wife was a former stewardess, a very beautiful woman. And because of that she had a lot of pride. When we got married, everyone said they couldn't believe what a good-looking pair of newlyweds we were. We had our reception in the Orchard Room at the Hotel Okura, a hundred eighty guests, but I guess that was the peak for me. . . .

"To be more specific, I look hard at the point when I lost control, but I still can't believe I became homeless. . . . Having passersby look at me like I'm something dirty. . . . I guess my life's hit rock bottom. . . . Am I gonna die on the streets?" On and on he went, sighing and weeping.

This man had been in Ueno for about six months, but then he packed up his hut and said he was moving over toward Toyama in Shinjuku. Rumor was that not long after, he'd been killed by some middle-schoolers.

In Tokyo, Yokohama, and Osaka, groups of youths were attacking homeless people for sport. Every time we heard another story, terror ran rampant through the people living in the park.

They'd been attacked with timber and metal bats, their huts set afire. . . .

Firecrackers had been thrown into huts, and then, when the occupants ran out, they had been set upon and stoned. . . .

The perpetrators had sprayed huts with a fire extinguisher, then ganged up on the occupants with air guns, signboards, and crowbars. . . .

And once the victim was exhausted from the violence of being kicked and punched, the perpetrators would set off fireworks at their face from a short distance until they went blind and then stab them repeatedly. . . .

———·———

REFERENCE NUMBER:

NAT 2 UENO PARK MANAGEMENT OFFICE

IMPROVEMENT WORKS ENDING: AUG 2012

Belongings of the homeless from the tent village must be bundled in tarps and secured with string, and each bundle must have attached a tag bearing a reference number, an identifying abbreviation and number designating its owner's usual "turf," like a license plate on a car. NAT is for the National Science Museum, SAI is for Saigō, LAN is for the lanterns at Ueno Toshogu Shrine, SUR is Mount Suribachi. Shige and I had lived in SUR, in the shelter of the trees at the base of Mount Suribachi.

- Attach (put on) to a visible (can be seen) part of the exterior (outside) of your baggage (belongings).

- This number (tag) cannot be borrowed or transferred (given) to someone else.

- Do not look after (watch) other people's belongings (bags).

- Put only necessary (needed) items in your bag, do not overfill (make it too heavy).

- You will be informed (told) in Aug 2012 of the next improvement (making things better) works.

The attempts to make the sign easier to read actually made it more difficult. I guess they must have thought that most homeless people barely had an elementary-school education.

The birds were calling to each other in the trees over the tent city. The occasional sound of wings flapping suggested that they were fighting, perhaps over food or because one had gotten too close to another's nest.

One little tent's blue tarp had become slack, and a few days' worth of yellowish rainwater and fallen leaves had collected on top. If the roof was flat, the tarp would get damaged and the cardboard that formed the hut itself would get sodden and disintegrate from the rain, so the golden rule was to create a sloped roof, but—

Next to the hut there was a bicycle with hangers and an umbrella and a hose and a bucket and all sorts of household essentials hanging off the front basket, handlebars, and rack. A child's yellow beach sandal with fingerprint-like traces of wear was caught in a rope holding up the tarp, and the clothes hanging on the bamboo broomstick protruding from the hut were women's underwear.

The tarp serving as a door curtain peeled back, and a white head emerged, belonging to the old woman who had talked about Shige's being found dead in his tent.

She smacked her lips together, *pa-pa-pa-pa*, as if speaking in baby talk, then started walking. On her right foot, she wore a sandal, on her left a white Adidas running shoe with the laces done up properly.

A man wearing a blue cook's hat jogged through the red torii of Hanazono Inari Shrine. He must've been a cook at one of the nearby restaurants, but I wondered which one.

The old lady, without giving a glance at the cook or the shrine, went down the gentle slope toward Shinobazu Pond, arms swinging as she went. Her upper half was bundled up in a gray down jacket with a pink vest layered over it, but on her lower half she wore only light purple trousers, perhaps having left her skirt in her tent. The left leg was torn from the hem, laying bare the oversize socks she was wearing.

She stopped in front of the vending machine in the middle of the hill and pulled two fifty-yen coins and three ten-yen coins from her pocket, counting them in her palm, then grasping them tightly as she looked up at the machine, muttering, "Hmm, hmm, hmm." She pressed one of the buttons underneath a little sign that read COOL and then, grunting as she bent over, pulled a plastic bottle of Amino Supli from the slot.

Dangling it from one hand as if it were heavy, the old woman went back up the slope, her expression unreadable.

At the bottom of the hill was the path to the zoo.

A tall, thin homeless man walked toward the main road, pulling a handcart after him. It was loaded with six semi-opaque ninety-liter garbage bags full of aluminum cans, probably three thousand yen's worth.

His long hair, mostly white, was tied back with a rubber band, his T-shirt was yellow-green, and his trousers might have once been gray but had nearly lost their color from being washed too many times. His brand-new black socks looked as if they were floating.

At the entrance to Shinobazu Pond, there was a taxi stand with about ten cars waiting in a line. About fifteen or twenty feet from the taxi, at the end of the line, a blue tarp had been spread out with about four or five hundred aluminum cans on top of it.

In the twenty or so plastic checkout bags tied to the railing separating the road and the pavement were someone's daily necessities, hung there for storage. The handle of a damp umbrella was hooked over the top of the rail, and a bamboo broom was stuck through as well. A blue tarp covered a trolley laden with blankets, clothes, pots, and more, and on the handhold of the cart, plastic shopping bags full of rope and work gloves and pastries were attached with laundry pegs.

A homeless man, head resting against the rail and legs stretched out between the rows of cans, looked vacantly out at the cars passing before him; then, he had apparently fallen asleep, his head slipped from the railing.

When I'd lived here, I had never been driven this far out.

Two large new signs had been put up at the edge of the park:

FUTURE WORLD HERITAGE SITE:
THE MAIN BUILDING OF THE NATIONAL MUSEUM
OF WESTERN ART HAS BEEN RECOMMENDED
AS A UNESCO WORLD HERITAGE SITE.

JAPAN NEEDS THE POWER OF DREAMS NOW
MORE THAN EVER. BRING THE 2020 OLYMPICS
AND PARALYMPICS TO JAPAN!

Would we be targeted for reduction once the foreign commissioners in charge of World Heritage listings and Olympics selection committees caught sight of the homeless's tents?

Shinobazu Pond connected to the cormorant pond inside Ueno Zoo, but the concrete-block wall around the Benten Gate exit had barbed wire strung on top.

Sometimes I could hear the sound of birdcalls from the zoo. One would start calling, and then the rest, unable to hold back any longer, would join in.

There'd be a splash, the sound of water, and I'd look at the surface, but the turtles and carp would be sticking their heads out, and I wouldn't be able to tell what had made the sound.

There was a group of white and brown ducks, some weaving their way through the lotuses, some resting with their bills on their backs, others floating upside down with their heads submerged, or beating their wings, scattering drops of water. The ones I thought were white ducks had hooklike curves at the end of their yellow bills. If they were some kind of seagulls, what sea might they have come from? Maybe Tokyo Bay . . .

Under a willow tree with branches extending into the pond, ladies in their early sixties leaned against the fence and conversed.

"Don't you think there are fewer sparrows about these days?"

"Some people catch them, as a job, I heard."

"What? Really?"

It was without doubt the two ladies who had been in the roses exhibition talking about Takeo. Both had black leather bags on their shoulders, tightly permed colored hair, and they wore neutral colors, shades of white, black, and beige. In their height and style of dress, they were almost too similar; perhaps they were sisters or cousins.

At their feet a pigeon puffed out its neck, cooing as it paced around and around trying to obstruct a male's or a female's path, but the two women looked out at the opposite shore of the pond.

"Someone told me they saw grilled sparrow at a restaurant."

"Oh, look, aren't those sparrows there? They've come back. Above you!"

A flock of sparrows descended from the sky as if they'd been scattered by someone, splitting in two directions in the trees, settling in a willow and the cherry tree next to it.

"Oh, no, one of them got me. It looks like it's going to rain anyway—shall we head off?"

They crossed at a light that had just turned green and walked up the slope past the vending machine.

A young man with a shaved head wearing a white running top and black leggings with bright red running shoes.

He crossed Tenryū Bridge, then stopped in front of the water basin at the entrance to Bentendo Temple. Taking the dipper in his right hand, he scooped water from the engraved stone basin and cleansed his left hand, then changed hands to cleanse his right, finally washing his mouth. In front of the offering box, he clapped his hands together in prayer for a moment, then ran at speed past the group of stone monuments for objects that have no further use, his back heaving with every breath as he passed the monument for eyeglasses, for the remains of eaten blowfish and softshell turtles, for folding fans, for bicycles, calendars, kitchen knives—

The young man took a thousand-yen note out of his waist pouch and bought an ema at the shrine office, then wrote a wish on the wooden tablet in black marker ink and hung it up with the others.

THANK YOU, GOD. I FINISHED THE MARATHON.
PLEASE CONTINUE TO LOOK AFTER ME.

He wiped away the sweat pouring from his face with a

towel slung around his neck and read some of the wishes written on other people's ema.

When I was young, I had no interest in other people's hopes or setbacks, but in his dark eyes, under those determined, straight eyebrows, I saw a clear sense of concern.

PLEASE GIVE ME GUIDANCE ON HOW TO GET LOTS OF
STUDENTS IN MY ENGLISH CLASSES.

MAY WE GROW CLOSER AND BE HAPPY TOGETHER.
LET US ALWAYS BE THERE FOR EACH OTHER!

PRAYING FOR SUCCESS AT MY AUDITION ON JULY 6.

IN THANKS FOR MY LOTTERY WIN.

PRAYING FOR A SAFE MOVE.

MAY MY FAMILY BE HEALTHY AND SAFE.

PRAYING FOR CERTAIN SUCCESS IN THE JAPANESE-
LANGUAGE TEACHER EXAMINATION THIS YEAR.
I'LL STUDY HARD.

PRAYING FOR MY DAUGHTER TO WAKE UP.

TO CHANGE STRESS INTO A FORM OF ENERGY!
TO BECOME A REAL MAN WITH LEADERSHIP!
TO FOLLOW THROUGH ON MY INTENTIONS!

LET THE YAKULT SWALLOWS WIN THIS YEAR AT LEAST.

PRAYING FOR MOM AND DAD TO GET BETTER.

Once he had read most of the ema, the young man put his hands on top of his head and stretched toward the sky. Then, his red running shoes kicking up the gravel of the path, he ran off past the oden stall at the foot of Tenryū Bridge.

FISHING PROHIBITED—CITY OF TOKYO

PLEASE DON'T FEED THE BIRDS, CATS, OR FISH.
—SHINOBAZU POND BENTENDO

On the south side of Tenryū Bridge, along the metal fence around Shinobazu Pond, there stood some huts that were little more than cardboard enclosing a small space

lined with more cardboard and blankets. Tents were not allowed to be put up around Shinobazu Pond. Previously,
when the management had been a little more relaxed, people had fished and caught ducks and cooked together
around an open fire here, but now the police and park officials made rounds, and the residents of the apartment
buildings nearby would call to make complaints to city hall.

To be homeless is to be ignored when people walk past
while still being in full view of everyone.

As I approached the huts, the acrid smell of cat piss hit
my nose. A striped cat in a red collar emerged from a cardboard hut, glued to the feet of a homeless man wearing a
black raincoat with the hood up. The cat looked a lot like
Emile, Shige's cat. The man stuck out a gnarled hand and
said, "Hey, Tiger," and the cat meowed in response. "You're
a good cat, Tiger," he said, patting the cat's head, and the
cat arched its back.

The wind was blowing, rippling across the surface of
the pond and rustling the branches of the willows, and
along the path around the pond, multicolored umbrella
flowers burst into bloom.

Tiger's owner looked up at the sky and shrugged.

"Looks like rain," he said, opening a green umbrella and

holding it over the cardboard. "Don't want to get wet and catch a cold, now, do we? Come inside." He picked up the cat and brought him under the umbrella, and the cat licked him roughly in the hollow beneath his Adam's apple. His owner's bearded face cracked a smile, exposing his crumbling teeth.

Rain—

It rained all night long that day.

At dawn it intermittently started to fall harder, and I was awoken by the sound of it hitting the tarp over my hut.

The cold had gotten into my socks, and both my feet felt paralyzed.

I didn't have to look in a mirror to know that my face was swollen and that my eyes were bloodshot.

I was exhausted after spending several days looking for somewhere in the park to die, and I'd already been here nearly five years.

The winter was always hard.

Unable to sleep at night because of the bitter cold, I would leave my hut in the afternoon in search of a sunny spot where I could curl up like a cat and nap. Those days were so miserable I'd almost forget that I'd ever been part of a family.

And that day it was a particularly rough morning, one that made me think living itself was a misery.

A notice had been posted on the door of my hut.

Pursuant to the following, please move
your tent and belongings.

DATE: NOVEMBER 20, 2006, RAIN OR SHINE

TENT TO BE MOVED FROM THIS LOCATION BY 8:30 A.M.

(NO ACCESS TO THE PARK BETWEEN 8:30 A.M. AND 1 P.M.)

1. All belongings behind the Tokyo Metropolitan Festival Hall, alongside the temporary railings and Cherry Blossom Road, and all belongings and tents behind Mount Suribachi must be moved in front of the fence behind the management office.

2. All tents and belongings near the statue of Bauduin, Sōgakudō Concert Hall, the former main entrance of the zoo, the trash-collection point, and the monument to General Ulysses S. Grant must be moved in front of the 'ghost lantern' near Seiyoken.

3. All tents located near Shinobazu Pond and the boathouse must be moved to the Shinobazu central path.

4. All tents near Saigō's statue must be moved to the side nearest the station, and all belongings must be put where tents previously were.

5. All belongings in the nursery near Seiyoken must be moved to the area designated with cones near the 'ghost lantern.'

6. After clearing up your tent, please do not leave behind dangerous items (batteries, crowbars, metal pipes, knives, etc.) or wood, etc.

—Ueno Park Management

That particular day was the day the officials were going to carry out what they called a "special cleanup" and what we called "chasing out the quarry." We were to pack up our huts and get out of the park before members of the imperial family came to view the museums and art galleries.

And the rain continued to fall—

Sticking an arm out of the blanket, I brought my watch to my face and saw that it was a little past five. It was a Seiko wristwatch that Setsuko and Yoko had bought me for my sixtieth birthday.

"Well, I'm not working anymore, and the most I'll be doing is going to the fields. What do I need a watch for anyway? We got a clock in the house," I'd said, unused to receiving gifts and not knowing how to accept one.

"I wanted to give you something you could wear, so Yoko and I went up to Sendai together and chose a watch, one we thought looked most like you. I know you don't need to worry about time anymore, but I thought you don't have anything of your own. . . ."

She'd been wearing something bright, orange or red, maybe. The color reflected well against her bushy white hair. I don't remember what exactly she was wearing, a heavy winter sweater or a light button-down shirt or what. But her clothes were as bright as a paper lantern.

Before I took the watch from its box and put it on, I looked at the grandfather clock. It was five minutes faster than the watch, and it chimed to let us know it was five.

"Well, that's the dinner bell," Setsuko said, and stood up. I heard her walking off toward the kitchen. In the six months since I'd been home, we'd spent every day together from morning till night, and I'd started to be able to tell by sound what she was doing and where in the house, even if I couldn't see her.

I stared at the black hands of the watch. This watch was a gift from Setsuko, but I thought of it as a memento of her. And if I was going to die on the streets like this, if anything might serve as a means of identifying my body, it would be this watch. They had gone to Sendai together, mother and daughter, to buy it, so Yoko would likely remember it. Had she filed a missing-persons report? And the house in Yazawa . . . my granddaughter, Mari . . . was that wiener dog Kotaro still alive?

Tossing and turning, thinking I should get up now, I fell back asleep and dreamed that I was standing on the bathtub in the house in Yazawa, in my sandals, trying to get out the window. The moment I got both feet up on the window frame, one of my sandals fell into the bathwater. I was unsteady where I stood, so I could not turn back to look at her, but I sensed Setsuko standing below, naked, ready to get into the bath. I yelled to her, "Oh, look at that!

The bathwater's all mucked up. Now how are Kōichi and Yoko supposed to get in that?" I awoke at the sound of my own voice. Suddenly the dense clouds of moisture hanging in the bathroom dissipated, and I was struck by the reality that this was not my house in Yazawa and that Setsuko and Kōichi were dead. Returning home in a dream isn't the same as returning home in real life. Imagine walking into my home in filthy shoes and then trying to run out the bathroom window . . . Could I really still resent Setsuko when I'd lost her so suddenly? . . . I looked at the watch as I listened to the sound of rain drumming against the tarp. Five thirty . . . fine, time to get started.

It was the twelfth of November, the fifth eviction in a month. There were lots of museums in and around Ueno Park, and members of the imperial family often paid visits to exhibitions and events there. The path of their vehicles took them past the Masaoka Shiki Memorial Baseball Field, but the reason we were forced to remove our huts from areas not even visible from the road was likely a scheme dreamed up by the Tokyo city government. The intent was to force out the five hundred homeless living in Ueno Park in order to win their bid for the Olympics. This was obvious, since we were unable to put our huts back up until a good few hours after the imperial family were back in their palaces, and when we returned to our original spots after night had fallen, we would find signs and fences and flower beds designed to keep the homeless out, forcing us to wander the streets. All of this I knew, but whenever there was an imperial visit, rain or snow or typhoon, I still had to pack up my things and leave the park.

Shige had explained it to me. "There are three kinds of imperial visits: one is when the emperor visits, another is when one of the crown princes visits. And then there's the third kind, a combination of the two. Emile, I'm writing a letter of appeal, so when that black imperial car comes, you can jump out just like Tanaka Shōzō and say, 'I have a request for Your Majesty!' Not even a police officer would try to arrest a cat," he said, scratching Emile under the chin. Emile stretched toward the sky, rubbing his mouth against Shige's fingertips.

They wouldn't tell us ahead of time what type of visit it was or who was visiting. The earliest notice was a week in advance, although sometimes they gave us as little as two days' notice.

I could take down and pack my hut up in two hours if I didn't stop for a break, but it took nearly half a day to reassemble. More difficult than the time and effort involved were removing the blue tarps and disassembling the cardboard and pieces of wood that served as walls and a roof, only to see in an instant that all my belongings looked like nothing but a pile of trash. The materials that made up my hut—the tarp, the cardboard—were all things that someone else had once thrown away.

That day I started dismantling everything at six in the morning, and by the time I had loaded everything up on a handcart, with a blue tarp over it to keep the rain off, and attached the number tag to it, it was past eight.

I watched the rain fall on the white patch of ground where my hut had been, turning it darker and darker until I could no longer tell the difference between it and the rest of the ground. Then I opened my umbrella and set off in the rain.

I hadn't yet decided where to go. Those with the means could, on these rainy winter days of exile, go to a manga café or a capsule hotel and have a shower and sleep, or spend the day in a sauna like it was a day off. Some people put the heaviest of their things into a coin locker at the station or one of the free lockers in a pachinko parlor and just rode around on the Yamanote Line all day. When the trains weren't busy, they could sleep in the warmth of the cars and go around gathering up magazines left on the train or in the trash cans on the platforms. . . .

But on that day I'd been feeling bad for a few days already, enough to make me wonder if I'd come down with something serious without realizing it. My stomach and back hurt very much. I didn't want to go out in the rain. I wanted to stay cocooned on my futon, if I could.

Even with my umbrella up, the rain blowing sideways against my face and shoulders hit me as if I were being stoned. Raindrops ran down my eyelids, and I could not see much in front of me. Breathing through my mouth like a dog, I wiped the rain from my face with my arm, but the sleeves of my coat were already soaked. The rain seeped through my clothes down from my collar to my back, and a chill rose from the nape of my neck, creeping its way into a headache. The need to pee was exceeding the limits of my endurance. I put all my energy into every muscle in my body so as not to stumble and fall, gripping my umbrella, step after step, headed to the public toilet.

There I took a piss, and although I hadn't meant to look, I saw my face reflected in the mirror over the sink. My damp hair was stuck down to my scalp, but I could see that I was going bald in the front and on top, and the few hairs I had left were mostly white. That wasn't all that age had touched. The corners of my body, too, were aging. Before, I wouldn't have been shaky in this sort of cold. When I left home at age twelve to work in the fishing port and slept on the boat, or when I worked on construction sites for the Tokyo Olympics, however cold I was, I'd never been so cold that I couldn't hold my fishing net or pickax.

I began to tremble slightly in my wet coat. I put up the collar and arranged the front, but the trembling didn't stop. To distract myself from the cold, I stamped my feet, and as I did, I heard a sloshing in my boots, and I knew then that the rain had gotten all the way through them. I hadn't fallen into a ditch, so there must be a hole in the soles.

When I left the public toilet, the rain had not changed, but the sky seemed just a little bit brighter.

A homeless man wearing a clear plastic raincoat from a convenience store was pushing a fully loaded cart with both hands, heading from the park management office to the designated safekeeping area.

A man in a green cleaning uniform picked up some bit of rubbish from a puddle and put it in a bag.

From the direction of the Ueno Station park exit came

some young people with backpacks and instrument cases on their shoulders. Headphones on under their umbrellas, listening to music, sharing an umbrella and chatting—they were most likely students at Tokyo University of the Arts, located down the main path through the park right past the Metropolitan Art Museum.

A man on a bicycle riding through the park, umbrella in one hand, a woman out walking her dog in the rain. The dog, clad in a red raincoat and hat to match its owner's, toddling through puddles, was the same type of dog as Kotaro, the dog my granddaughter owned. We usually called him Kota, calling him by his full name only when he was in trouble. "Kota, sit, give me your paw, good boy! Kota, this minced meat cutlet is good, isn't it? Konno in Haramachi makes great cutlets. . . ." "Granddad, don't give him fried food! Dachshunds have short legs—when they get fat, they get intervertebral hernias, so we have to keep an eye on his weight. Kota, you can't sit next to Granddad at dinner anymore." Oh, that's right, Kota was a dachshund, wasn't he . . . ?

As I walked down the central path, one of the park's garbage-collection trucks drove past, splashing me with muddy water and soaking my pants.

A ten-ton Tokyo Metropolitan Symphony Orchestra truck was parked by the Tokyo Metropolitan Festival Hall, and under the building's overhang there was a rusted blue bicycle parked on its stand. An old homeless man sat on a folding stool holding an umbrella. A big white cat was curled up on his lap. Its face was dirty with eye discharge and mucus; its tongue lolled from its mouth. It didn't seem like it had much longer to live. On the ground next to the bicycle was another umbrella laid open, with bread crusts scattered underneath and a number of sparrows picking at them.

Down Chuo-dōri from the direction of Ueno-hirokōji came a phalanx of about ten riot-police vehicles, a transport van at the head, followed by the bomb squad's equipment and the explosives-disposal vehicle, and an evidence-collection vehicle, which would film any trouble and save the footage.

I looked at my watch. It was 8:57. The riot-police vans stopped in front of the big fountain at the plaza; the police got out of their transport vehicles and opened their umbrellas one by one. Officers from the forensics department's canine unit, clad in dark green uniforms and hats and wearing tall rubber boots, started walking their bomb-sniffing

German shepherds around the undergrowth of the park to make sure that it did smell only of undergrowth.

At 9:32—one hour after the deadline to leave the park—I walked down the slope by Hanazono Inari Shrine and stood at the foot of Tenryū Bridge by Shinobazu Pond. The surface of the pond rippled with each raindrop that fell, the ripples spreading out, then disappearing, rippling, then disappearing—where do they go? I wondered, but then, as if my very core had been pulled out of me, I could not stop shaking, as if I were trembling at every single drop of rain that dampened my shoulders.

Suddenly the countless streams of rain interrupting my vision as I stared at a withered lotus flower appeared like a big black curtain—clearly showcasing my life, closed off with nowhere left to go. Even though the curtain's come down . . . why wasn't I getting up from my seat . . . ? What more did I think there was to see . . . ?

I was now, I realized, walking the path around Shinobazu Pond, used in the Meiji era as a horse-racing track, the Meiji emperor himself a spectator. The path was wide, the umbrellas of people passing well apart as they walked on. I couldn't hear the beating, breaths, voices, just people, people, people, rain, rain, people. . . .

I remembered a rainy New Year's Eve and how much I loved the sight of the people of my hometown passing on the stone steps at Hiyoshi Shrine, tilting or half closing their umbrellas as they wished each other a happy New Year. Time had passed, things had moved on, yet events I should have forgotten soon after they happened stayed with me, trailing behind me. . . .

I saw some bright red coin lockers, and my eye caught the sign for Ueno Star Movie, known among the homeless as the little porno theater. In one building there were three theaters: Star Movie, which showed double bills of old films; Japan Masterpiece Theater, which specialized in your average pornos; and World Masterpiece Theater, which specialized in gay porn.

For five hundred yen, you could sleep in a soft seat in a warm theater until the last screening ended at around 5:00 A.M., so more than a few made use of the little porno theater during rainy midwinter days when we could not stay in the park.

I went in. Four or five seats at the back were filled. All the occupants were homeless, but none lived in Suribachi like me. Each residential area in the park had its own territory, and though we didn't really stand around and chat or drink together or have any kind of neighborly relation-ship, we'd keep an eye on each other, keeping watch to make sure no intruders came close. We had a loose sense of camaraderie.

I sank down in the middle of the very front row and looked ahead. The title of the film was *Hubby Swap: Lusty Busty Wives*. Although all I usually had to do to go to sleep was simply close my eyes, that day it was impossible. Some-thing inside me was pushing away the need for sleep.

Behind me I heard loud snoring, and—was someone drinking?—the smell of sake drifted toward me. Someone was beating his head left and right against the back of his seat, occasionally heckling, "You bastard," "Idiots," "Fuck you!" Nobody was watching, but the projector rolled on.

A husband who works for an adult-toy company wants to know what his products are like to use, so he gives his wife one of their vibrators. She uses it, then demands that her husband make love to her, but he's so tied up with work that he cannot satisfy her desires. The husband's immedi-ate superior's wife is also in endless agony. The two women wait until their husbands have gone to work, then open up to each other about the slumps in their respective mar-riages. They hit upon the idea of swapping husbands—

Watching the projected images of naked men and women intertwined on-screen, I no longer had any idea what I was seeing. There was a throbbing pain behind my eyes, and I was hit by the soured smell of my own sweat, to which I had paid little attention outside or in my hut. A chill came over me, sweat began to seep from my every pore, and acidic bile began to rise up into my mouth. One belch could bring it all up, so I stood, stooped over, and ran out of the theater.

The rain now fell as if it were whispering softly to each of the passersby hiding their heads under their umbrellas; it was not cold enough to turn to snow, yet the cold was strangely intense.

I walked. The cold and my headache were tied up with each other and seemed like something I could push away on my own, but only my feet moved forward, forward. I hadn't made a clear decision to do so, but I felt as if I were heading toward the library that Shige had mentioned to me.

When I started to cross the road, the crossing light turned red. I looked at my watch. It was 12:29—the "special cleanup" notice had said we were forbidden from the park between 8:30 A.M. and 1:00 P.M. I had never returned to the park before the restrictions ended. But if I went back, would I be doing any wrong? What would be the violation? What harm would it do, what would I encroach upon? Someone might be bothered, someone might be angry? I was doing nothing wrong. The only thing I was guilty of was being unable to adjust. I could adapt to any kind of work; it was life itself that I could not adjust to. The pain of life, the sadness . . . and the joy . . .

Going up the escalator, I saw the newest entrance to Ueno Station, built in 2000 when the Panda Bridge was unveiled. Next to the Panda Bridge ticket gates, there was a ten-foot-tall panda doll in a clear acrylic case. The flow of people over the bridge was sporadic. The fact that I could see only the hips of people passing me and the rain puddles made me realize that I was walking hunched over, looking at the ground, like a prisoner being marched off for committing a crime—

A pigeon stopped on the railings three feet ahead and craned its neck at me. Seemingly used to being the subject of people's gaze, the pigeon alighted at my feet, and then, when I was nearly close enough to tread on it, it took just a few hops off to the side and did not try to fly away. Maybe one of the homeless had been feeding it on bread crusts or something—on sunny days homeless people would sit against the metal fencing on the overpass and eat or sleep, but today there was no one.

I saw a single black BB fall into a rain puddle. Was there a child somewhere with an air gun hunting homeless people sleeping in the open? Taking aim at the people waiting on the platform for the next train?

Under the overpass were the platforms for the Utsunomiya Line, the Takasaki Line, the Jōban Line, the Jōetsu Line, the Keihin-Tōhoku Line, and the inner and outer loops of the Yamanote Line.

A homeless man had jumped from Panda Bridge onto a train and killed himself, or so the police had said when they came to the tent village to ask questions. The guy had lived in the group of tents across from the National Museum of Nature and Science, but nobody knew his name, birthplace, or anything by which his body could be identified, nor was there anyone who would speak. They hadn't found any trace of the life he'd lived outside Ueno Park.

Crossing Panda Bridge, I climbed a set of stairs, and there was the park. It had not been taped off, nor were there any announcements being played. Everything in the park continued as always, the same as any other day. The people passing through on their way to work or school at their usual time might not even have noticed that no homeless person sat on the benches or that the blue tarps and cardboard huts had been removed. It wasn't their homes that had been cleaned up; they weren't the ones who had been chased out of the park. . . .

They didn't even notice the police officers asking a young man questions near the Masaoka Shiki Memorial Baseball Field; or the officers, half in plainclothes, half in uniforms, waiting along the main path; the plainclothes officer standing guard under the overhang of the National Museum of Western Art; or the helicopter circling low over the park.

Then the plainclothes officers gathered in front of the Tokyo Metropolitan Festival Hall, pulled a black-and-yellow-striped tape across the path so that pedestrians could not cross, and began explaining to people walking from the station and the zoo.

"This path is closed for the next ten minutes. Those who are in a hurry should go around the park, please."

Seeing passersby carrying their umbrellas at their sides, I realized that the rain had stopped.

It was 12:53.

"Is something going on?" a man who must've been a

student, dressed in jeans and a duffel coat, asked an officer in a suit.

"The emperor's vehicle will pass here soon."

He was a short, stout man with a buzz cut, more suited to frying noodles at a street stall than being a detective.

"Yeah? It's our lucky day! The emperor!"

"The emperor?"

"Awesome. The emperor! Might as well stick around to see him, right? Is he coming soon?"

"Shouldn't be long now."

"Damn! Where's my camera? I gotta take a picture for my mother."

"Which side of the car is he gonna be on?"

"This side. The empress will be on the other side."

"Oh? And why is the emperor coming past here?"

"Their Majesties attended the ceremony for the International Prize for Biology at the Japan Society for the Promotion of Science."

A white police motorcycle appeared from the direction of the National Museum of Nature and Science. I looked at my wristwatch; it was 1:07.

The motorcycle passed, followed by a black car. The imperial car was approaching.

It was a Toyota Century Royal with the imperial standard, a gold chrysanthemum with sixteen petals, on the hood. There was also a gold chrysanthemum in place of the license plate.

There they were in the back. Just as the officer had said, the emperor was seated behind the driver, and the empress was on the passenger side.

The nearly thirty people who happened to be there by chance waved at the vehicle or held up their phones, uttering in surprise, "It's really them!" "They're so close! Like six feet away!" "Just like on TV!"

The imperial car, which had been going about ten miles an hour, slowed to the speed of a leisurely walk, and the rear window rolled down.

The man who waved tremulously, palm toward us, was the emperor.

The empress waved to the people on the other side of the road; then, leaning forward in her seat, she turned to greet us with a graceful wave of her pale hand.

The emperor and empress were a stone's throw from me. The pair gave us a look that could only be described as gentle, and smiles came across their innocent faces, ones that had never known sin or shame. Because they were smiling, one could not see what they were really thinking. But they were not the same kinds of smiles given by politicians and celebrities, ones meant to hide their feelings.

A life that had never known struggle, envy, or aimlessness, one that had lived the same seventy-three years as I had—we were both born in 1933, I'm certain of that, so soon he would be seventy-three. And his son, the crown prince, born on February 23, 1960, was forty-six—if my son were still alive, he'd be the same age, too. Born the same day as Crown Prince Naruhito; we borrowed one of the characters from his title for the name of our eldest son—Kōichi.

Only tape separated me and Their Majesties. If I ran out toward them, I was sure to be snatched by police, but they would see me and hear me if I said something

Something—

But what?

My throat was empty.

As the car went on into the distance, I waved after it.

He had heard my voice.

On August 5, 1947, Emperor Hirohito had appeared, wearing a suit, as he stepped down from the imperial train that had stopped at Haramachi Station, and the moment he put his hand to the brim of his hat in greeting, I was one of the twenty-five thousand voices that cried, "Long live the emperor!"

At the age of thirty, I decided to come and work in Tokyo, and I worked on the construction sites of the Olympic stadiums. I didn't see a single event, but on October 10, 1964, sitting in my small room in the prefab company dormitory, I heard the voice of the emperor through the radio.

"I declare open the Games of Tokyo celebrating the Eighteenth Olympiad of the modern era."

And on February 23, 1960, when my wife, Setsuko, was going into labor, the radio announcer had said exultantly:

TODAY AT FOUR FIFTEEN THIS AFTERNOON,
AT THE IMPERIAL HOSPITAL, A PRINCE WAS BORN.
MOTHER AND CHILD ARE BOTH DOING WELL.

Suddenly my eyes filled with tears. I strained all the muscles in my face to stop them from falling, but my shoulders began shaking with each breath, and I hid my face in my hands.

Behind me I heard the sound of someone dragging his feet. I turned and saw a homeless man, dressed in a coat that was too long and walking on the backs of his shoes like they were slippers. Another pushed a cart full of luggage covered with a blue tarp, his umbrella dangling from one hand.

I saw the police get into a patrol car and leave the park. The exile was over.

I could smell the rain now. The scent of rain was stronger just after it had stopped. All of Tokyo is covered in asphalt, but in the park there are trees, earth, grass, and fallen leaves, and the rain brought out their fragrances.

In my thirties, I did overtime every night. As I walked to the station, I'd be overcome by the waves of salarymen on their way back from work, and I'd wonder if they had families waiting for them at home, and on nights after it rained, I walked in my muddy boots over the wet asphalt, shimmering with reflections of neon signs, and then I could smell the rain—

Some sunlight pierced through the clouds to the west, but to the east the sky was still so heavy with rain clouds that it looked as if it might start again at any moment.

I heard a burbling sound, and I looked toward the

Tokyo Metropolitan Festival Hall, but I couldn't tell whether it was water coming out of the gutters or circulating inside the air-conditioning system. With my head turned toward the sky, breathing in the smell of rain and listening to the sound of water, I realized exactly what I was going to do next, like a moment of enlightenment. I'd never used the word "enlightenment" before. I was not getting caught up in something and going along with it, nor was I running away from anything, as if I were a sail allowing itself to be pushed forward by the prevailing wind—suddenly I didn't care anymore about the cold or my headache.

The yellow of the ginkgo leaves poured into my eyes like paint dissolving into water. Each leaf had a golden glow that was almost too beautiful—the ones that danced in the air, the soggy ones trampled on by people, and the ones that still clung to their branches.

Since I became homeless, my only interest in ginkgoes was the fruit. Wearing plastic gloves, I picked them up one by one and put them in a plastic bag. When it was full, I took them to the water fountain and washed off the part of the skin that stank. Then I would spread them out on a newspaper to dry before taking them to Ameyoko Market, where I could get seven hundred yen a kilo for them.

My vision was filled with yellow leaves, whirling in the cold winter wind. The turning of the seasons no longer had anything to do with me—but still, I didn't want to take my eyes away from that yellow, which seemed to me like a messenger of light.

The chirp of the signal for the visually impaired was what made me realize that the light had turned green.

I crossed the road.

I took some change out of my pocket and bought a ticket.

I passed through the gates at the park entrance of Ueno Station.

A sign with the words NORTHEASTERN SHINKANSEN SERVICE—SHIN-AOMORI BOUND came into view, and suddenly I thought if I took that train, I'd be at Kashima Station in four and a half hours—but this hesitation lasted only a beat. The feeling of homesickness no longer made my heart pound or my chest tighten.

A number of paths were now behind me.

Only one way was left before me.

Whether it was the way home or not, I wouldn't know until I tried.

I took the stairs down to Platform 2, the inner loop of the Yamanote Line.

A woman almost ran into me on the stairs. A petite woman in her thirties wearing a red coat with a shiny bob like a little girl's . . . She was coming up the stairs, staring at her phone, and just before we collided, she looked up. "Oh, sorry," she said, her face pale and lifeless.

In the flash of surprise that registered on her face for a moment as she realized I was homeless, I saw a shadow, as if all her dreams had just been crushed. I stopped and turned around near the bottom of the stairs, just in time to see her red coat disappear. Now she wouldn't witness anything, I thought, and felt a little better. I wondered if she'd just gotten some bad news on her phone, but most likely she'd sleep well tonight, and in the morning she'd wash her face, have something to eat, do her makeup, get dressed, and leave her house. And her life would continue. The calendar separates today from yesterday and tomorrow, but in life there is no distinguishing past, present, and future. We all have an enormity of time, too big for one person to deal with, and we live, and we die—

I watched one train go past, down the inner loop of the Yamanote Line. In the three minutes until the next train arrived, I bought a carbonated drink from a vending machine and took only two gulps before putting it in the recycling bin.

THE TRAIN NOW APPROACHING ON PLATFORM TWO IS THE IKEBUKURO- AND SHINJUKU-BOUND YAMANOTE LINE TRAIN. PLEASE STAND BEHIND THE YELLOW LINE.

I stood on the yellow line and closed my eyes, leaning my whole body into the rumbling sound of the approaching train.

My heart pulsated as screams tore through my body.

My field of vision turned crimson, green spreading through it in ripples.

Rice fields . . . watered, freshly planted, this year's rice paddies . . . in the summer you have to weed it daily or else . . . lilies and rice look a lot alike, and they'll suck the nutrients from the rice, so you have to pay close attention . . . the green of the rice paddies behind me now that I'm flying . . . I'm on a train? . . . oh, it's the Jōban Line . . . going from Haranomachi to Kashima . . . the Niida River . . .

I bring my face up close and look at the river . . . a silver fish I can see 'cause its tail fin's moving so fast it's in time with the flow of the river . . . and in the spring a group of young sweetfish coming back to the river from the sea . . . the dazzling light falling on the fields by the riverside . . .

Each moment is brilliant and charged with shadow. Everything that appears in my eyes is too bright and too clear. I felt not that I was watching the landscape but that I was being watched by it. Seen by each of the daffodils, dandelions, the butterbur flowers, the spring starflowers—

As if my body, now walking, was being pushed along by the wind, I soon knew I was walking on the beach. The monotonous sound of the waves along with the scent of the tide filled my nasal cavity. Unlike the wind and the rain and the smell of flowers, the scent of the tide stuck to my skin like a spiderweb.

I was walking on Migitahama, a beach I had known since childhood, and yet, as if I'd entered somewhere I wasn't allowed, I glanced up at the sky from beneath the brim of my straw hat.

There was the sun.

I turned back and looked.

Footprints in the damp sand.

I squinted and looked at the sea.

Where the sky and sea met, it was smooth as steel, but where the sea and sand met, the waves broke white and tiny foam bubbled up, the shells and seaweed and sand that had just been engulfed now gasping for breath.

Occasionally a breeze came in from the sea, rustling the branches of the pines, bringing forth the smell of the needles heavy with pods, stroking my cheek like a warm sigh.

I followed the wind with my eyes as it left, watching, then realizing that there was Kitamigita, the village where I was born and raised.

It shouldn't have been visible from the sea, but I could make out the roof of my house clearly.

The sky was blue and taut, but near the horizon I saw a large, spotlessly gray layer of clouds.

A flock of seagulls squawked, springing from the pines all at once, then flying off as if riding on the wind.

A sound like a jumbo jet taking off rumbled, and a moment later the earth shook.

I saw a telephone pole wobble like the mast of a ship going out to sea.

I watched as people ran out of a plastic greenhouse, crawling on their hands and knees through potato patches, crying out, holding each other, clinging on to their trucks.

I saw pollen fall from the shaken pines, turning the air pale yellow.

I saw concrete-block walls crumble, roof tiles fall, manhole covers float, roads crack, water gush.

The emergency sirens blared over and over.

"A tsunami warning has been issued. Expected arrival time of 3:35 P.M. Waves of up to twenty-three feet are expected. Please seek shelter on higher ground."

Police cars and public-safety patrols came speeding toward the sea, sirens blazing, yelling out over their loudspeakers, "Tsunami coming, get to safety!"

Above the breakwater, people who had been watching the horizon line of white waves get ever closer suddenly, as if repelled, ran away shouting.

The tsunami swept over the pines, raising clouds of dust as it rolled up boats, smashed into trees, washed away fields, tore through houses, crushed gardens, swallowed up cars, felled gravestones, ripped apart roofs and walls of homes, glass from windows, fuel from boats, gasoline from cars, tetrapods, vending machines, futons, tatami, stovetops, desks, chairs, horses, cows, chickens, dogs, cats, men, women, the elderly, children—

There was a car driving down Highway 6.

My granddaughter, Mari, was driving, and in the passenger seat was Kotaro, the dachshund.

She parked in front of a house and got out, grabbing the chain of a Shiba Inu who had been leashed to a doghouse in the garden. Obviously taking charge of another abandoned dog. She picked up the dog and got into the car, slamming the door shut. The moment she started the engine, a black wave appeared in the rearview.

Mari gripped the wheel and stepped on the accelerator, sliding onto Highway 6 still in reverse, but the black wave chased the car, then swallowed it up.

Carried out by the tide, the car holding my granddaughter and the two dogs sank into the sea.

When the breath of the tide calmed, the car was enveloped in the light of the sea. Through the windshield I could see Mari's pink uniform from the animal hospital. Seawater in her mouth and nose; her hair flowing with the waves appeared brown in one light, black in another. Her wide-open eyes had lost their sight, but they shone like black slits. Just like Yoko, she had long eyes, taking after

Setsuko. Kotaro and the other dog both died in the car with her.

I could not embrace her, nor touch her hair or cheek, nor call her name, nor cry out, nor let tears fall.

I looked at the swirl of her fingerprints on her right hand, already starting to swell and turn white, still grasping the dog's lead.

Little by little, little by little, the light faded and the ocean calmed as if sinking into a coma.

As Mari's car melted into darkness and I could no longer see it, I heard, from inside that darkness heavy with the weight of water over it, that sound.

People wearing all colors of clothes, men, women, seeped out of the darkness, and flickeringly a platform emerged.

THE TRAIN NOW APPROACHING PLATFORM TWO IS BOUND FOR IKEBUKURO. PLEASE STAND BEHIND THE YELLOW LINE.

YU MIRI is a writer of plays, prose fiction, and essays, with over twenty books to her name. She received Japan's most prestigious literary award, the Akutagawa Prize. After the 2011 earthquake and tsunami in Fukushima, she began to visit the affected area, hosting a radio show to listen to survivors' stories. She relocated to Fukushima in 2015 and has opened a bookstore and theater space to continue her cultural work in collaboration with those affected by the disaster.

MORGAN GILES is a Japanese translator and reviewer. She lives in London.